STOLEN SECRETS

Elizabeth Alsobrooks

Stolen Secrets

By Elizabeth Alsobrooks
© 2017 Stolen Secrets
5714 Peri St.
Swartz Creek, MI 48473

Tell-Tale Publishing Group, LLC

TT Imprint

Elizabeth Alsobrooks Imprint

For my Irish-Scottish husband, Kenton, who knew I was a writer and loved me anyway. A fan of both blarney and myth, he has nothing against chasing a good story or adventure, so happily accompanies me in my pursuit of both.

CHAPTER ONE

Everything about the shop was irregular, including the displays which projected at odd angles, supported by ornate wooden brackets and the occasional book case or other Egyptian artifact. Its merchandise had been collected and added to over a lifetime of adventures, and the result was vastly eclectic and often mismatched and even mysterious. The windows of the cluttered antiquities dealership, not yet shuttered, allowed slanted sunlight to illuminate dust motes, thick and insidious, seeking every crevice and ornate feature in which to drift. Brushing her hand across the table to clear it of its most recent layer, Isabella unrolled the map and traced the route with her fingertip.

She heard the bell above the front door jingle, waited for the expected greeting, and sighed. Five minutes later and Misha would have arrived to clean and bar the entrance, and then she could begin preparing for the dig of a lifetime. This incredible new commission would reward her with financial independence and the ability to pursue her genetically-transmitted archaeology passion full time. No more being stuck in this dusty little means of survival. Besides his addiction for archaeology and her impoverished but noble lineage, this was the only other inheritance her father had left her.

She had loved her father, but she was sick of eking out a living selling trinkets to tourists. If she could spend more time in the field, she might actually have something valuable to sell, too.

"Hello, anyone around?" a deep male voice called in Arabic, from the front of the shop.

"Coming," Isabella replied in the same language, rerolling the map and tucking it into a pocket of her skirt before hurrying through the hanging Persian rug labyrinth that served as a hallway of sorts, separating her office cubby and storage space from the main display floor. She emerged into the showroom to greet the latecomer, and continued, "How may I help--" Surprised, she stopped for a moment, then quickly added, "May I help you?" Her customer was an incredibly handsome man, though that wasn't the most surprising thing about him. He was in fact the second attractive visitor to enter her establishment that very day, but this one she recognized. She had seen him around Cairo in the past. Never up close, and not in person, but she knew *of* him. Who didn't? *What is he doing in my lowly little shop*? Isabella wondered.

"There you are," said the tall Bedouin, flashing straight white teeth worthy of a dental ad, which contrasted beautifully against his tanned skin and the Indigo-dyed blue of his robes and kuffiyah, which matched his startlingly blue eyes, Isabella noticed with further surprise. "Lady Isabella Valentine? I've come to offer you an incredible sum, in either gold or British pounds, your choice, for the most exciting archeological dig you have ever been on!"

"W-what?" She glanced toward the door and noted two more Bedouins, standing sentry on either side of the entryway. More, she knew, would be outside, no doubt tending to the beautiful black stallion of Prince Mukhtar, eldest son and heir of Sheikh Abdul Kummel al-Rahman, Leader of the Hassana. The gold agal of his kuffiyah might as well have been a crown, but the entourage he traveled with assured his identity could not be mistaken.

"Forgive me, Lady Valentine," he replied, this time in flawless English. "Allow me to introduce myself."

She held up her hand, and said, "No need for that, Prince Mukhtar. Everyone in Cairo knows who you are. But please do explain what you're talking about."

He bowed his head politely, and took a step closer. Looking down at her, he said softly, "Of course, My Lady, with pleasure. I wish to procure your services as an archaeologist. I seek this," he said, pulling a drawing from somewhere within his robe and extending it toward her.

She took the drawing, happy to distract herself from the intensity of his stare, the penetrating azure gaze that both took her breath away and made her want to gasp in gulps of air to fuel the manic beating of her heart at his nearness. Then, recognition made her inhale slowly, as she willed herself to remain outwardly calm. She looked up and said, "May I ask why you're seeking this?"

"So you *are* familiar with the piece," he said as fact and not a question, and the small smile he bestowed upon her matched the warmth in his voice as if she had just passed some test at which he had hoped she would excel.

"Yes, of course. Most in my field would recognize *The Chalice of Isis*. But you didn't answer my question," she persisted.

"I have a buyer with bottomless pockets, of course. And do you know where it is located?" he asked, small dimples appearing in his cheeks.

"I'm afraid I can't help you," Isabella said, handing him back the sketch.

He made no move to accept it, but instead chuckled, a rich, deep timber that made her smile in response until he said, "Now you have not answered *my* question," and she wished she had just shared an intimate joke so they could become better acquainted instead of parting company.

"My services are already engaged, which is why I'm not at liberty to say," she said softly, lifting her hand and waving the sketch at him.

He reached out to take the paper, but instead of accepting it, he clasped her hand and cradled it within his own. Something flickered in his eyes. *Disappointment? Annoyance?* But then he was smiling again, and she moved her hand, only to have him grasp it more firmly and say, "I've come too late to hire you? No matter. Let me assist you, then. I don't need the item itself, just a copy of the reverse side, the emblem that is missing in this sketch, in all sketches of the object."

"What are you suggesting?" Isabella asked. "I thought you just said you had a client who would pay anything to get the chalice?"

"The chalice itself isn't essential, if it's already sought by another. What we seek is the symbol not revealed here in this sketch. It may be a missing key for the interpretation of another artifact."

"Oh. I honestly don't know if that's a possibility or not. I can speak to my client and discover whether or not they object to what you suggest," Isabella said, managing to pull her hand free, and burying it in the folds of her skirt. She took a step back. His request seemed perfectly innocent, but she was convinced it was anything but transparent and she couldn't think straight with him gazing into her eyes like that. He was so close she could smell the appealing aroma of rich espresso with cinnamon he enjoyed recently. It was her own favorite after work pick-me-up.

"What more could I ask of you, Lady Isabella? You're most gracious. I'll return tomorrow for your answer," he said. Before she could think of a response, he turned and hurried from the shop, his men on his heels.

She stared at the door long after the bell stopped jingling, and wondered why so many people were interested in this particular relic. How'd they even know she'd just bought the map to its whereabouts? One was a coincidence, but two in the same day meant trouble. Big trouble, and more secrets than she, in her excitement over this morning's hefty paycheck, had bothered to investigate. What had she gotten herself into?

The door flew open and she jumped, then relaxed once she recognized Misha. "Hello, Misha," she said.

"Good evening, Lady Isabella," Misha said, turning to bolt the door behind her, before crossing the shop and disappearing into the carpet labyrinth, seeking cleaning supplies.

Isabella reached into her pocket and pulled out her cell phone. She needed backup.

CHAPTER TWO

What else could I do? The Usurper got to her first," said Mukhtar, raising his voice to be heard above the tinkling bells on camel bridles, bleating goats, and the reverberations of sprayed sand against the outer walls of the pavilion.

The cool night winds whipped against the goatskin sides of the tent, bellowing smoke from the inner fire up the chimney flaps high above their heads. Shadows played across his father's chiseled features, illuminated by firelight as they sat cross-legged on cushions, relaxing after a bountiful feast provided for the benefit of their honored guest. The darkness prevented him from gauging his father's emotion. He disliked disappointing him, for he respected this man he loved, this man whose men followed him with blind devotion due not to his wealth and position, but because of his fearless prowess as a soldier and his wise and just leadership abilities.

"The queen is going to be displeased that you were unable to secure the woman's map, or at least her services," said his father thoughtfully.

"Wait, Abdul, we don't have to involve my mother yet," said Prince Anubis. "After all, Mukhtar may still be able to plant himself in Lady Isabella's party."

"That's already been taken care of," Mukhtar agreed quickly, relieved that Queen Isis wouldn't be notified that his mission was a failure until he had time to rectify the situation. "We have men asking around and insinuating themselves into the dig site crew and the caravan, seasoned workers, some camel handlers and suppliers. Their resumes are glowing and their references flawless. With the number of men we have seeking positions, we will dominate her entire party."

"And you? I'm sure you took the opportunity to push your charm on the beautiful Lady Isabella? Did she seem inclined to accept your individual help with terrain and territorial permissions?"

Mukhtar shrugged, uncomfortable under the focused attention of Prince Anubis. His family had served the immortals for many generations, by choice not enslavement. They fought a common enemy, the evil Usurper, Set, an immortal god who with a small entourage and immediate family members had separated from the rest of his royal family thousands of years ago and was determined to enslave mankind for his own nefarious purposes.

"Surely she gave you some indication," Anubis pressed.

"I'll discover the effect of my visit tomorrow," Mukhtar said, unwilling to project an outcome that hinged more on Set's interference than his interaction with the fair-haired foreign beauty. He had yet to fully consider his surprising reaction to the exchange himself. His desire to accompany her, if he were honest, was more than a quest to fulfill his mission.

"Did you meet the Usurper's agent?" his father asked, pulling his thoughts from the memory of Lady Isabella's full lips and lush figure.

"There was no sign of him, father. Apparently the man came in and procured her services earlier in the day. How could they have found out she had the map that quickly?"

"That's exactly what my brother is trying to find out," Prince Anubis said. "There had to be a leak."

"I still don't understand how that seedy little artifact peddler managed to slip through my men's hands. They sighted him on the outskirts of town just before dawn, then lost him. By the time they caught up to him again, he was already on his way out of her shop. He didn't have anything on him. Apparently she bought everything he'd stolen from that dig site. He sells to her a lot, specializes in an assortment of minor antiquities and upscale touristy trinkets. She had no reason to suspect this lot was stolen."

"At least we know Lady Isabella isn't involved," his father said.

"Which means she's in extreme danger," Mukhtar reasoned, "and needs to be protected, not just used for her skills as an archaeologist."

"All the more reason for you to insinuate yourself into her good graces," the immortal prince said, smiling broadly. He stood, towering to his full height of 6' 6" and Mukhtar immediately rose to face him, wondering if he had revealed his attraction to Lady Isabella by expressing concern for her safety.

Mukhtar crossed his arms over his heart and bowed his head in a gesture of respect to the immortal prince considered by many to be a god. But to indicate his own respect for Mukhtar, Anubis extended his hand. Mukhtar clasped it. Prince Anubis' robe slipped back from his forearm to reveal a glimpse of the golden symbol, gleaming like molten sunlight within the bronze skin of one of the true Illuminati's inner circle. It was just for an instant, but it was the first time he had seen the tattoo-like symbol up close. It was every bit as amazing as rumor claimed.

"I have no doubt you'll find a way to help us retrieve the artifact and save the beauteous damsel as well, Prince Mukhtar," he said, nodding his head toward the Sheik who now stood beside his son. "My brother, Ljluka, will quickly discover who betrayed us. Once we know who Set's operatives are on this venture, we will get them out of your way. Whatever you need, just let Luc know. I would accompany you, but my mother has need of me in Brazil first. Her absence should give you time to take care of this matter."

"Your trust in me is well placed," Mukhtar said, relieved, despite himself, to hear that Queen Isis would be out of the country, giving him the time he needed to retrieve her artifact. King Osiris, he knew, had more pressing things on his mind and seldom troubled himself with his wife's interests unless she asked him to interfere or they directly involved him in some way—though rumor had it that he tried to keep informed of all his wife was up to, as past experience had taught him she was not always forthcoming with all she knew or orchestrated.

"Walk out with me, my friend," Prince Anubis said.

Mukhtar watched as his father and the immortal prince exited the tent. His father was not a small man, nearly as tall as his own 6' 3", but next to the lifelong friend he called Andrew when they were alone together, his father looked diminutive. He was glad to be on the same side.

Turning, he threw himself back down onto a cushion and reached to pour himself a fresh cup of coffee, piping hot and Turkish, with a hint of *asab*, sugarcane juice, just the way he liked it. Though he had to admit that as usual Hassidim, Prince Ljluka's valet and indispensable attention-to-detail guru, had been right to pass along that little spray scent for him to use. He had seen the subtle flare of her nostrils when he drew close enough for Lady Isabella to notice the aroma of her late afternoon addiction wafting from the edge of his *kuffiyah*. She had assumed, as planned, that they shared the same taste in coffee, and probably hadn't even realized the way she had leaned toward him after that, but he had. He almost felt guilty plying her with unspoken promises of espresso delights. Almost.

He took a sip and chuckled. Whatever it took, he was going to become invaluable to Lady Isabella Valentine, and if that meant smelling like her afternoon delight, so be it. The idea enticed him, too.

A vibration rattled his cup on the tray, and he reached for his cell phone. Noting the caller ID, he shook his head and answered, "You're uncanny. What? Never mind. You were right about the espresso. Did you find anything else that might help me?" Mukhtar glanced up as he heard his father reenter the tent. "Are you sure? Okay, thanks, Hassidim."

"Hassidim?" the sheik asked as he sat beside him on an adjacent cushion. He chuckled and said, "Any news from the hyper little man?"

"Apparently they've discovered proof of Set's involvement behind the man who acquired the services of Lady Isabella, and it was as we already suspected his minion who infiltrated the dig site where the Illuminati operatives uncovered the map. That's why they knew of the theft and managed to secure her services. The thief was following Set's orders and deliberately sold the map to Lady Isabella. They must have thought she would be easily manipulated and controlled, making it convenient as well as expedient."

"Who's the operative accompanying her on the dig?"

"That's another thing. We don't know. It's not one of Set's active agents, not one we've encountered before. Ljiuka is apparently continuing to investigate the man, but their early Intel points to him being a legitimate acquisitions agent, a well-known artifact wholesaler from the United States. His parents immigrated there when he was a young boy." Mukhtar reached for a date cookie sprinkled with sesame seeds from the plate a serving girl had just placed on the low table between them. He took a bite as he waited for her to exit the tent, then continued. "They own and operate an auction house in New York City, and specialize in museum quality artifacts. This is not the first time he's involved himself in the hands-on acquisition of a particular piece. He may have been hired by Set without even knowing his actual identity or the purpose for which Set is trying to obtain the chalice."

"This complicates things for us," his father said, accepting a cookie from the plate his son held out toward him. "What's his name?"

"David Khourey."

"Khourey? A common name. He could have a lot of relatives here. I will send out a few of my own men to investigate any possible connections. I'm sure they are already having the man followed, but doubling up his surveillance can't hurt, either. You should make his acquaintance. If you don't make headway with the lady, perhaps you can befriend her employer's agent. I'm sure he would be happy for safe passage across the territories through which they will be traveling in order to reach the dig site."

"Not a bad idea, father, but how I'll *accidentally* make his acquaintance is the question." Standing, Mukhtar pressed a number on his phone. "I'll need some more Intel myself if I'm to make this happen before they embark."

CHAPTER THREE

ome friendly advice?"

"Of course. Is something wrong?" said the man Mukhtar's men had identified as David Khourey, turning to look at Mukhtar.

"Not this company, my friend," said Mukhtar.

"No? May I ask why?"

"His vehicles are old, poorly maintained and mistreated. They will give you nothing but trouble."

"Really? They looked okay to me." David glanced at the paved but pitted lot behind the attention-grabbing neon sign that contained tightly parked Jeeps, Land Rovers and a few small compact cars. All were shiny and clean, a young boy scrubbing dust from a windshield demonstrating the reason for its gleaming appearance.

"From there," Mukhtar said, pointing to an establishment further down the road. "They're maintained by family. Each vehicle even has a name and a personal mechanic. And should you have a flat or another unforeseen problem, you won't open a trunk or tire carrier only to find another flat or missing crowbar. The dash compartments contain maps with marked Oasis stops and a small first aid kit.

There's also a small tool chest aboard each vehicle, as a courtesy. They cost a bit more, but their actual value is much higher."

"I see," David said, nodding his head and looking at the wooden, neatly hand-painted sign above the shop Mukhtar had indicated. "*Omar & Sons Rentals*. Not as secure sounding as *Safety First Transports*, but perhaps putting his name on the business means he takes personal pride in his reputation, as you say. It does seem like they have more reliable transportation and certainly a better managed inventory. Thanks for the advice . . ."

"Mukhtar. You will not regret it. In fact, you will see what I mean when you find the proprietor interviewing your fitness to commandeer his caravan rentals."

David laughed and held out his hand. "I look forward to that. My name is David Khourey."

Grasping it, Mukhtar said, "A pleasure. You've rented desert transports before?"

"Yes, but last time they had been procured before I even arrived. I wasn't sure exactly what I would need until the last minute, this time, which is why I am overseeing the details myself."

"Ah, a large job?" Mukhtar asked.

"An archaeological dig," the man said, looking past Mukhtar to where his men were idly waiting behind him, next to his Land Rover. As if he considered Mukhtar to be a fellow merchant seeking to form a caravan, which was actually Mukhtar's intent, he said, "Say, do you suppose you could point me in the right direction for some tools and supplies I've not been able to get on such short notice? Plenty of merchants can order them, but I need them by tomorrow morning, if possible."

"That is a problem. One can find anything in Cairo if they know the right people, however, so today is your lucky day. I happen to know all those right people."

"Fantastic. I thought you might. So you're forming a convoy as well? You must let me compensate you for your time though."

"Your Highness, your father is on the phone for you." Moto held out his phone. "You left it in the vehicle, my prince," he added with a slight bow.

"Thank you, Moto. Excuse me," he said to David, turning away and walking off a few steps, pretending to speak to his father on the phone. Moments later, he ended the supposed call, and walked back to where David waited.

"A Prince? Forgive me. I didn't mean to insult you by offering to pay you for your services."

Mukhtar held up his hand and said, "No, no, no offense was taken. As a matter of fact, I'll let you repay me by taking me to lunch. I was about to go to the Concorde El Salam for lunch. They have marvelous Turkish coffee and allow me to stable my horse there when I am in the city. Give me a list of your needs and I will have one of my men contact the appropriate merchants. The suppliers will come to you, rather than you wasting your afternoon seeking them out. Where are you staying?"

"Believe it or not, I am staying at the Concorde El Salam. This couldn't be better. I'd be happy to buy you lunch, as well as your companions. Please, my car is just there," he said, pointing to a black Jeep a short distance away. "Would you like to meet me there now?"

"What a marvelous coincidence," Mukhtar said, feigning surprise. "My pleasure," he confirmed, smiling with genuine satisfaction, glad his plan was working better with David than it had with Lady Isabella.

***

Seated across from the antiquities dealer, Mukhtar nodded at the right moments during the retelling of the man's previous archaeological adventures and took the opportunity to study his adversary more closely. He was sure Lady Isabella found the man attractive. His strong jaw even sported a chin dimple like the one that movie star all the ladies adored had. Wide brown eyes, intelligent and lively, currently reflecting his enthusiasm for treasure hunting, revealed even more reason for the lady to find his company appealing.

David laughed as he described the reaction of a crew member who had a near-fatal encounter with a tomb's theft deterrent system, one of many well-known booby-traps used by the ancient pyramid architects. Mukhtar laughed in response and realized the man's natural charm was going to give him some serious competition in winning the attention and trust of the beautiful English rose any man would find alluring. And despite this knowledge, he actually felt himself liking this Egyptian-born American with his quick wit and open personality. He hoped the man was as innocent as he seemed, and his motives as transparent as presented.

"Did you have any problem gaining the permits and territory permissions for your journey?" Mukhtar asked casually.

"Territory permissions?"

"Yes, for the occupied territories you will need to cross in order to arrive at your dig site. Some of the regions you are crossing are owned by tribes not . . . shall we say, welcoming, to strangers. Foreigners on their land is all the incentive they need for violent confrontations."

"Violence? Do you mean they would actually attack us?" David asked. His brows furrowed and he took a long drink of his coffee, clearly troubled by Mukhtar's revelation. "It seems I may need another item, Prince Mukhtar. Weapons. Do you know where I might obtain some, discreetly?"

"It's not enough to have guns. You need men capable of using them, and it's also still advisable, no, necessary, for you to obtain permission to cross certain regions *before* you get to them."

"I wonder if Lady Isabella knows about this," said David.

"Did you say Lady Isabella? Not the owner of *Aladdin's Treasures*, that eclectic little tourist trap in the marketplace?"

"You know of her?"

"Know of her? You're not going after *The Chalice of Isis*, are you?"

Surprise registered on David's face. He glanced around the table at the other two men, Mukhtar's companions, and said, "Was my meeting you just a coincidence, Prince Mukhtar? Or were you deliberately trying to ingratiate yourself to me?"

"Deliberately? I assure you it was no such thing. I was there on an errand for my father."

"So you're not the man who wants to accompany us on the dig and wants to acquire a photograph of the symbols on the chalice?"

"Now that I will most certainly not deny." *Damn, so she has already told him*, Mukhtar thought, trying to decide on a way to salvage the situation.

"Then how," David said, standing to confront him, "do you expect me to believe it was mere coincidence running into you?"

"How was it not?" Mukhtar said, standing to face him. "Lady Isabella never divulged your identity."

"Well . . . it is the greatest of coincidences then," David said, running his hand through his hair, obviously confused.

"Indeed," agreed Mukhtar. "May I ask what your answer was? Were you willing to let us accompany you, assisting you further in your acquisition of the artifact in exchange for a copy of the back side symbol?"

"Oh. Well, I saw no reason to deny you, unfortunately my client has declined your offer and is instead sending his own men to assist us."

"He is sending men?"

"Yes. I wonder. Now that I think of it, he said it was a security team. At the time I thought his intent was to protect the relic once we acquired it, but after what you have suggested, I'm not so sure. I-I thank you for your help, Prince Mukhtar, but I really think I had better go make a few phone calls."

David extended his hand and shook Mukhtar's warmly enough, assuring Mukhtar that the man might not completely believe his story, but had been somewhat reassured by his quick explanation. He smiled and nodded, then watched as the man hurried toward the exit.

Glancing at Moto, he said, "Let's go. I have a meeting in the marketplace I need to get to."

***

The bells above the door jingled as it closed behind him, and Mukhtar watched as Lady Isabella turned, clipboard in hand, from where she had been counting small busts of Ramses II. Today she was wearing khaki pants tucked into ankle-high boots, belted below a matching and equally serviceable-looking khaki sports shirt, boasting multiple pockets and hints of curves that had been much more noticeable in the gaucho skirt and silk blouse she had worn the day before. The pleasing classical symmetry of her face paraded a variety of emotions before she settled upon a neutral one of patron greeting a customer, lips turned slightly upward, and she said,

18

"Good afternoon, Prince Mukhtar. I hear you have met David and know the answer to yesterday's inquiry, so I am rather surprised to see you here. Was there something else I could help you with?" she asked, setting the clipboard down on the shelf and walking down the aisle to stand before him.

"Lady Isabella, it is always such a great pleasure to see you," he said, smiling down at her upturned face. "Your client's refusal does nothing to eliminate my need to persuade him on my own, but that is not why I have come. After having met, as you say, your partner for this venture, the most pleasant and personable Mr. Khourey, I have come to express my concern for the safety of both the relic and you yourself, my dear Ms. Valentine."

"My safety? Whatever do you mean?" She took a step back, and by the way her jaw tightened, he could tell she was affronted. No woman ever ground her teeth like that in mild displeasure, though he couldn't help wonder what she did when she experienced extreme pleasure. "I assure you that Mr. Khourey has been nothing but polite and gracious and I am not such a dim-wit that I didn't have him properly vetted, and his credentials, I assure you, check out." She emphasized her indignation by planting her hands upon her narrow waist, and had she stomped her foot he would have lost his composure altogether and laughed aloud.

Holding his hand up to forestall such a gesture, he said, "You misunderstand me, My Lady. Forgive me. I didn't mean to imply you were in danger *from* Mr. Khourey, but perhaps you may be in certain dangers *because* of him."

Her head tilted to the right, a mannerism he had already noted signaled contemplation from the petite spitfire. "What do you mean, *because* of him, but not *from* him?"

"To be more specific, because of his inexperience in acquiring all you need for safe passage both to and from the dig site, let alone while you are engaged in the actual hunt. Without my intervention earlier, he would have rendered you stranded in overheated piles of junk in the middle of the desert rather than rambling toward your destination in worthy endurance vehicles. Given your line of work, I'm sure you have obtained the necessary government permits, no doubt through one of your friends at the university or on the museum board, but are you aware of the tribal unrest and territorial rifts that have recently occurred?"

Her eyes darkened as she glanced away. Chasing her doubt, he added, "Where even a fortnight ago it was safe to travel, it is no longer advisable even for a heavily armed team of professionals. I am worried that without my help you may never reach the dig site, let alone obtain the artifact. What good would my procuring your benefactor's permission do me, and I firmly intend to do so, if you don't accomplish your mission?"

"What is it you're suggesting?" she asked, her lips set in a firm line as if already knowing and prepared to deny his request to accompany her.

"You know who I am, but did you know that a vast majority of the region you wish to cross belongs to my father, and that huge tracks of it also belong to me or one of my relatives, however distant they may be?"

Her eyes widened with obvious surprise. She opened her mouth, then closed it again, moving her hands from her hips to knead them nervously. "Did you tell Mr. Khourey that?" she asked suddenly.

"I never got the chance," he admitted. "I'm not threatening to halt your venture if you refuse my aid, Lady Isabella. I'm merely pointing out what a huge asset I could be to you. And as far as protection is concerned, which you always need in the event that a band of thieves overtakes your caravan, or even your dig site, you know I have the trained men necessary to provide the kind of security you will need. Who knows what other treasures you might uncover during this expedition?"

"I had thought of that, of course, but David, that is, Mr. Khourey, assured me that his client is providing security and a team will be here by tonight. So you see, it seems that even if as you say Mr. Khourey doesn't have the experience necessary to equip this venture, his benefactor does. So if you are not here to threaten me with trespass, and you claim you are not, I feel I must again decline your kind offer, Prince Mukhtar. If and when you do gain permission from the client who is already funding this venture, I will be happy to revisit your offer."

"As you wish, Ms. Valentine," he said, his smile masking his disappointment. "I look forward to seeing you again soon." He reached down and grasped her hand, pulling it to his lips. Kissing the top of her hand, he released it and winked before turning to hurry out the door Moto held open.

CHAPTER FOUR

sabella let her breath out and cupped her hand over the place his lips had caressed. His lips were full and warm, and no doubt used to brushing against feminine flesh. She knew she should feel relieved that he wasn't going on the expedition with her, but couldn't deny the disappointment she actually felt.

"Was that Prince Mukhtar I saw leaving?" Misha asked, startling her from her daydream.

"What? Oh, yes, he seems determined to accompany us on the dig. I hope I was able to convince him that he is not needed or wanted. David said our boss was quite clear that the prince was not to be involved."

"A pity, if you ask me, Miss. What woman wouldn't enjoy his company around the campfires at night, or benefit from the protection of that small army he commands?"

Isabella didn't lie to Misha or herself by disagreeing. "It doesn't matter. The man who's paying for the expedition says he's out, so he's out. I need that paycheck," she added, reminding herself why she must stay focused on the prize. A vibration accompanied by a low buzz drew her attention, and she reached into her pant pocket to retrieve her cell. She noted the caller. "Hello, David. I was just talking about you. Yes. Yes, he just left. Did you know the majority of property rights on our trek belong to him and the sheik, or some of their relatives?" David was as surprised as she was, which didn't make her feel reassured. "He told me so himself, but he promised he would not interfere with our journey. Yes. Well, he did insinuate that there had been some recent unrest in the territories and we may experience danger." She tucked a stray strand of hair behind her ear and listened to David's offer to hire some mercenaries he'd heard about. Shaking her head as if her caller could see her negative response, she said, "I think you'd better get in touch with our boss and see what he says about it. Yes, okay. I'll call one of my friends at the museum, too, and see what I can find out."

She thumbed the end call button and pressed star, then one, on her way to the back of the store. The phone rang four or five times. When the beep sounded, she sighed and said, "It's me. I need to talk to you ASAP." Sitting down at the table, she flipped open her laptop and clicked on a bookmark that brought up a current territory map of the region she was most concerned about. It wasn't large, perhaps twenty kilometers across, but it might as well have been hundreds, as far as it was from the nearest modern civilization. They had satellite service the entire trip, but that didn't mean help could reach them if they needed it, at least not before it was too late.

She had managed to steer clear of the flesh peddlers thus far, not a matter she took lightly in his part of the world given some of the dangerous situations in isolated locations she'd been in, and she had no intention of breaking her perfect record now. The prince's warning bothered her more than she liked to admit, because she knew the existing, underlying dangers he was too diplomatic to list, knowing she would understand what was involved when a female was intercepted by hostile forces in the middle of the desert.

She gnawed at her bottom lip and pulled open the bottom drawer of the file cabinet to her left. She reached in and picked up the *Lady Smith*, the 357 revolver her friend Elsa had given her for her birthday last year, dubbing it the best silent partner money could buy. It fit snuggly in her hand, but the nice heft of the fully-loaded piece always felt comforting in the cargo pocket on the right thigh of her pant leg, as easily accessible as a holster. She retrieved a box of shells and slid them into the left pant-leg pocket before reaching for the small scimitar and thrusting it into her waistband.

"What's all this? I thoughtcha weren't off 'til first chirp?"

Isabella gasped and swiveled her chair to better face the doorway. "Elsa! A good thing that dagger was sheathed or you might have made me perform an appendectomy on myself."

"I see yer still jealous Disney has seen fit at long last to make a princess cartoon about me too," said the laughing redhead, plopping down on a loosely covered crate, overflowing with curly spirals of wood wool packing material.

"I wouldn't be so quick to laugh if I were you. Plenty of chaps were calling you an ice princess long before Disney got wind of your wiles," Isabella countered, joining in her friend's laughter.

"Ha! Just for that, I should keep this lot to myself," Elsa said, brandishing a steaming takeaway cup from which Isabella caught a whiff of cinnamon espresso.

"Oh, you wouldn't dare! I give!" she said, accepting the cup gratefully and taking a tentative sip to gauge its temperature and savor its flavor. "Mm," she said with appreciation. "No wonder you're my best friend."

"And don't I know it? I've nipped a full ten-day holiday for you."

"What? You're coming? Don't jest."

"Use 'em or lose 'em the old geezer was warning me just a fortnight ago. I'd been like to pop up to see me mum, but I'd far rather this exploit with you. No reason you should tuck off with all the best man flesh in Egypt all to yourself, then."

"It's not that, trust me," Isabella said, suddenly serious. "I think it's going to be more dangerous than we thought. I was just trying to reach you to tell you about it."

"Ma hands were a bit occupied at the time. Give it, then. What are you on about?"

"The prince was just here and--"

"Oy! See what doing a favor has cost me? I missed his royal hunkiness!" Elsa reached out to grab hold of Isabella's arm. "Promise me that I get to ride with him!"

"No one's riding with him. Boss's orders. Sorry." She patted Elsa's hand and pouted her lips with feigned sympathy. "Now come here," she said, getting up and shoving her chair toward Elsa before grabbing one sandwiched between the file cabinet and some upright, rolled Persian rugs. She pushed it up to the table in front of her laptop and sat down. "Look here." Isabella pointed to the territory she suspected was in current chaos. "Didn't you say this chieftain had recently died? From what the prince said to me there's new infighting and territory disputes on our route, and I suspect it would be here, if anywhere. Do you think there's a way for us to bypass this territory?"

Elsa leaned forward, pressed her index and thumb against the screen and slid them apart until she had enlarged the map to display a particular territory in detail. "The problem with that is we couldn't get a permit to pass through this bit here. It's government. There's a no trespass order in place. Dunno why, but that's recent too. Maybe they're related. Plenty of oil wells there."

"No wonder," Isabella said, sitting back and taking a long pull on her coffee.

"Hope this boss bloke can grease enough palms to make it doable."

"Me too. It may be our only hope. Come on, let's get out of here. Misha can close up. I need to get something to eat before I help you pack."

"Help moi?"

"Yes, you know as well as I do you haven't even started and I'm already packed. We need to hurry or we won't get any rest at all."

***

Isabella shifted the weight of Elsa's backpack on her right shoulder and fit the key into the lock. Once inside, she dropped it onto the floor and turned to disengage the alarm. Only the alarm wasn't beeping. No lights, green or red, were flashing, and the keypad digits weren't glowing from within. *No power?* She reached over to flick on the lights. The florescent overheads flickered and began to ignite. *So power is working.*

"Um, Izzie?" Elsa whispered.

Isabella turned toward Elsa. "Why are you whis--" she began, only to freeze once she realized the disaster at which Elsa was staring.

A heavy crash sounded from behind the Persian Rug labyrinth, followed immediately by a male voice cursing in Arabic. Elsa grabbed her arm. "We have to make scarce!" she whispered urgently.

Though giving voice to Isabella's instincts, she didn't have Isabella's affronted outrage over having her father's legacy burgled and ransacked by strangers. Waving her hand to indicate Elsa should stay put and be quiet, she dug in her cargo pocket and pulled out her silent partner. Time for her partner to contribute to the business in a meaningful way. She reached back to douse the lights. "Phone for the police," she whispered, then glanced down and thumbed the flashlight app on her cell before dimming it.

Knowing her way around the store better than any intruder was a huge advantage. Thankfully the thieves hadn't heard her or seen the lights go on, or they would have already responded. They must have shut her office door in order to turn on the lights without making them visible from the front of the store.

She crept down the aisle, careful to step over the shattered Ramses statues and display case glass. If she was lucky they may not have discovered the safe yet. It was hidden beneath a trap door in the floor under the table in her office, masked by a thick carpet. Only Elsa and Misha knew about its existence, or the fact that she kept some of her most precious relics there, the ones that were purchased through auction houses, like the one Elsa's brother worked for in London. Pausing at the entrance to the rug maze, she cocked the gun, took a deep breath, and soft-stepped down the corridor. She could make out low conversation now, and hesitated, not sure how many men might be crowded into her office or the small storage room beyond.

What am I doing? Isabella wondered. The door to her office opened and light spilled into the hallway. She pressed the app on her phone and turned off the flashlight, dodging into a small opening between carpets that gave them access to the broom and cleaning supply closet. Straining to hear, she pressed herself against the wall, hoping she was hidden in the shadows. She needed to know how many men she was up against. The element of surprise wouldn't help her if she was outgunned or vastly outnumbered.

"It's got to be here somewhere. The supplies are here, the road maps, everything. If it wasn't at her house, it's got to be here," said a man with a gravelly voice. Isabella stiffened, realizing these creeps had been in her little house, going through her personal belongings. The knowledge strengthened her resolve and she tightened her grip on the revolver.

"Maybe she's got it on her," replied a younger-sounding man. "You think she'll come back here tonight?"

"Izzie? Psst. Izzie?"

Isabella closed her eyes, willing Elsa to shut her mouth and run away.

"Guess so," Gravelly Voice said, much softer now. "Let's go."

Inching toward the carpet gap, Isabella saw a short man wearing a white robe and red-checkered kuffiyah pass by her hiding place, followed closely by the younger, taller version. She waited, but when it became apparent no more men were behind them Isabella stepped to the rug edge and peered out. Seeing no one, she stuck her head out and glanced back toward her office. The lights were still on, making it possible to see that the corridor was empty. Hurrying after the men, she rushed forward and jammed her silent partner into Young Man's back. He froze, as expected, and she reached around him to pull the dagger from his hand, relieved he wasn't carrying a gun.

"Stop where you are," she called to the other man. "Elsa, have you called the police yet?"

Gravelly Voice spun around, shining a torch in the face of Young Man. Isabella took the opportunity to shove the gun against the man's temple and said, "Put your gun on the floor and kick it toward the front of the store."

"No need to be so unfriendly. This is all a misunderstanding. We can work it out."

"I believe I already told you how you can work this out. Elsa!?"

"They'll be here any minute!" Elsa called. "Are you okay?"

"Turn on the lights!"

The fluorescents flickered to life and Isabella pressed Silent Partner more firmly against Young Man's temple. This is your last warning," she said.

"Father!" pleaded Young Man.

The chubby Arab bent down and placed the gun on the floor, pushing it toward the front of the store with this foot. "Okay, happy? Now just let us go. We didn't take anything."

"You took plenty. Do you think all the damaged inventory and display cabinets were free? At the very least, I expect you to pay my insurance deductible," Isabella fumed. "Now interlace your fingers and put them behind your head." Both men complied and she added, "Now get on your knees, and don't you dare move. I'm so angry right now I could shoot you out of spite."

"Okay, okay, just calm down, Miss. We are doing as you instructed," said Gravelly Voice.

Red lights flashed revolving beams into the store and then Isabella heard the front door bells tinkle, followed by the sound of Elsa in animated conversation with entering males.

"Isabella? It's the police. They're coming back to help you, honey," called Elsa.

A team of uniformed men appeared, clustered around the entrance to the Persian rug labyrinth. Taking in the situation, one of the officers said, "Well done, Miss." Pulling out his weapon, he pointed it at the thieves and added, "We'll take it from here. Please lower your gun, Miss."

Relieved, Isabella stepped away from Young Man, and gently released the hammer before shoving Silent Partner back into her cargo pocket. "His weapon is up there," she said, pointing to where the gun had been kicked against a cabinet across the room. "And here," she added, "His son had this."

She handed the dagger over to another officer who stepped forward to put his hand on her shoulder. "Are you alright, Miss? That was terribly brave, and probably a little crazy."

Chuckling at his attempt at brevity, she said softly, "I'll be okay now. Can you check to make sure there's no one else in here? They were in my office back there," she said, pointing behind her. "There's a storage room beyond, too."

"Of course. Why don't you go outside with your friend now, Miss. Omar? Come with me," he said. He and another office, apparently Omar, moved down the corridor, guns drawn. Without need of further encouragement, Isabella trailed the officers escorting the thieves outside. Elsa immediately threw herself at her, hugging her close, and she watched the officers push down the heads of the thieves as they loaded them into the back of their cruiser and sped away.

"Am I ever glad to see you," Elsa confessed, eyes sparking tears of lingering fear and profound relief in the flood lights the second cruiser had shone against the storefront.

The other officers emerged. "Are you the owner, Miss?" asked the officer she had sent into her office?

"Yes. Were they the only ones inside?"

"All clear. You're lucky. If they'd had more accomplices we might have come upon a much different scene. Here, Miss," he said, handing her a card. "It's late. You're probably tired and upset. We have another call, so get some rest and come down to the station tomorrow to give a statement." Without waiting for a response, he joined his colleagues, already getting back into their vehicle. Lights flashing, they sped away.

"What in hell? They're just going to leave us standing here looking silly?"

"Come on, Elsa. Let's go inside. I want to see how much damage they caused in the office. God I didn't need this mess now. We leave at dawn. I need to call Misha, too. I need the alarm company to come check out--" She turned toward the flashing lights.

"Oy, I knew it. They just had a dire one, and now the blokes will make nice and see that we're tuckered in snug as bugs. Come on. That dripper I got you last Yuletide still work? I'll whip you out a steaming cup of some such. That'll perk you, Izzie."

Three vehicles sped forward and parked, lights still spinning. Officers emerged, running toward them. "Are they still in there, Miss?" asked a police officer Isabella had never seen before.

"What? No. The other police officers took them off to jail," Isabella said, an uneasy feeling causing the hairs at the nap of her neck to tingle. "Didn't they radio ahead?" she asked, knowing the answer, even as Elsa grabbed her and pulled her back.

"Can we see some identification first?" Elsa demanded.

Badges were quickly presented, and Isabella sighed. "We've been burgled, vandalized and duped, all in one night, officers. We'd best go inside and try to figure out what's going on."

"Lady Isabella? You appear unharmed, thank the heavens. I have the alarm technician in route, and Misha is on her way as well. Is there anything else I can do for you?"

"Prince Mukhtar? Do you know the proprietor?" asked the officer Isabella had been addressing.

"Yes, Lady Isabella Valentine. Let's get her out of this cool night air, shall we?"

Several officers, who had immediately entered the business upon arrival emerged with yet another all clear, and as if he were immediately in charge of both the situation and everyone present, the police stepped aside to allow the prince to usher Isabella and Elsa into the store. One of his men appeared at his elbow with a cardboard cup tray filled with steaming beverages.

"You must be a bundle of nerve endings. Here," he said, handing Isabella a coffee that smelled surprisingly like cinnamon spiced espresso. "Earl Grey?" he asked Elsa, whose eyes grew as big as a tea cup before she nodded vigorously and accepted the heat-protection-sleeved takeaway. "And now let's find you somewhere to sit before you fall down from exhaustion and delayed shock," he said graciously, extending his hand toward the back of the store as though he were hosting high tea in his parlor.

Delayed shock, Isabella thought. *Yes, that and complete confusion and uncertainty,* she mused as she allowed herself to be ushered into her own office. Like an automated doll, she plopped into the swivel chair, sighed with relief when she noted the desk still atop the rug hiding the trap door to her safe, and the undisturbed laptop she was trying to recall having backed up onto a cloud over the last few months. She took a long swallow of the just-right espresso, sighed deeply and felt her shoulders slump from the aftermath of adrenaline overload, and the sudden realization that she was in way over her head in an escapade she had mistakenly thought would be a fun, profitable artifact retrieval. It left her feeling exhausted. *All the world's a stage, And all the men and women merely players; They have their exits and their entrances, And one man in his time plays many parts,* she thought wryly, drinking again from the warm cup she had clasped firmly between chill fingers. Her hands shook slightly.

She looked up and into soft blue eyes the color of an English sky in springtime. They seemed filled with tenderness and genuine concern, without even a hint of duplicity or guile. Such beautiful and intelligent eyes, focused upon her with eager intensity. A woman could lose herself in those deep blue pools. Many had, she was sure of it.

Somehow the prince had crouched down beside her and wrapped his arm around her shoulders before she was even fully aware of his presence. "Everything is going to be fine, Isabella," he said soothingly. "You're safe now." And even though she wondered how he had come to be here at this particular moment, and what part he was currently playing, she liked that he had used her name without the title, as though they were friends. She felt herself believe him, because she so desperately wanted to believe him, and she had no idea why.

CHAPTER FIVE

sabella came awake slowly. First she became aware of luxurious sheets and the soft feather down feel of firm support that can only be found upon a high-quality mattress. Next she smelled the distinct aroma of freshly brewed coffee and bacon. Yes, bacon and fresh baked goods. There were other enticing aromas, but she stretched languidly like a lazy feline, burrowing into the plush pillows. Then she heard voices and the distinct clatter of serving dishes and remembered where she was.

She opened her eyes. The glowing digits of the clock on the nightstand confronted her. Nine! She couldn't believe she had slept in that late. The room was still in darkness, save for the soft glow of the clock and the dim nightlight along the underside of the bathroom vanity that gleamed upon the highly-polished floors. She could see the white marble tiles and the rosewood of the vanity from the open doorway.

Her need to use the facilities coaxed her from her warm cocoon.

A quick check in the hidden pocket above the underwire of the bra dangling from the doorknob assured her the map was still neatly folded inside. She padded across the lush carpeting to the window. Pulling the heavy drapery aside, she revealed bright, mid-morning daylight and squinted, averted her face and let the curtain fall back. Late! Isabella rushed around the room, gathered her clothing and got dressed. Five minutes later, she secured her braided hair into an elastic hair tie, and threw open the bedroom door.

"I was a tick away from coming to see if you were living, or what, you lazy get. You look much better rested up though, Izzie. Come. The only thing missing is a bit of bubble and squeak, but they've brought mushrooms, beans, hash browns, bacon and even fried tomatoes along with some lovely poached eggs and hearty bread of some sort. It's almost like eating at me mums, a proper English breakfast. And do try some of this marvelous orange marmalade," Elsa urged, tearing a chunk of jam-dolloped bread off and stuffing it into her mouth.

'I wish you had tried to wake me, Elsa. I can't believe I slept so long. Has David called?"

"He did, and he's the reason you're just waking. He said I was to let you sleep as long as possible, because you needed to get your rest and that if you weren't feeling quite yourself when you did arise, we would postpone our journey until tomorrow."

"Really? That was certainly thoughtful of him."

"Oh, he's quite the gentleman, our Mr. Khourey. I don't recall you mentioning how suave and sophisticated he is, Isabella. Were you planning to keep him all to yourself?"

"He came in person? Oh dear. Let's eat then. I don't want to keep him waiting any longer. Are you packed and ready?" Isabella probed, reaching to fill her cup with sweetened Turkish coffee. She wasn't usually a big fan, but found it to be quite mild and smooth. It went perfectly with the thick slice of bacon she'd just devoured. She hadn't realized how hungry she was until she began eating. "And the prince?" she asked casually, forking a bit of egg onto a slice of toast.

"Wondered when you'd finally get around to our host."

She glanced over at Elsa, but only raised her eyebrow expectedly.

"Yes, you know he was here, in all his royal hunkiness, asked about your welfare, if we had everything we needed, if he could come rub gold leaf over the whole of your bod."

"Elsa!" she cried, but there was no helping the laughter her friend's teasing solicited.

After the laughter died down, she said, "You know, that robbery affected me more than I realized. After the hot soak in that enormous tub and that toddy you insisted that I drink, I was out the moment my head hit the pillow. I barely remember coming to the hotel last night."

Elsa jumped up and ran around the table to give her a bear hug. "Who can blame you, Izzie? I'm still not believing you confronted those monsters alone, now am I? The angels must be looking out for you overtime, love."

"And I can't believe we agreed to stay in his suite, but to tell the truth I couldn't bear the thought of going home to a burgled house and seeing if those creeps had been through my undies and what nots."

"Everyone wholeheartedly agrees with you, Isabella. The prince mentioned that your house had already been set to rights, and both places are now equipped with fully functioning state-of-the-art alarm systems, complete with monitored video surveillance." She raised her hand and said, "Nope, don't even say it. Your boss apparently paid for it. He seems to think they were after your map, the one you need to find his treasure. An entire platoon arrived this morning to escort you and his suaveness, and me of course, to the dig site."

So she had been right and the thieves were after the map. If her new benefactor knew it, too, that also meant he knew something about this artifact he hadn't divulged. She wondered if David knew. It seemed certain the prince knew. He seemed to know everything. Was he somehow involved in the burglaries? She downed her coffee and jumped up.

"Okay, Elsa, let's get moving. Let's find out what else my new boss has sent for us, and hopefully David will have more answers than questions today."

"A Humvee, David? Do you really think it's necessary? They're not the most comfortable SUV," Isabella observed, shifting her weight and uncrossing her leg, getting restless after six hours in the metal box.

"Perhaps. But I've been told they're the safest," he said. "And as to your earlier question . . ." He thumbed a button on his cell, and looked over at her. "Our employer has assured me that by the time we arrive at the territory in question he will have negotiated safe passage."

"That's a relief, though I have to say that I feel pretty guilty accepting the prince's help and then still refusing to let him accompany us."

"I don't disagree, but it's not our decision," David said, shrugging. "We got a late start today and you've had a rough couple of days. I feel like it's time to stop for the night. There's an oasis up ahead according to the map."

"Ugh. Thought you'd never ask," Elsa said, pulling her earphones out and shoving her phone in her pocket. "Me bum's been asleep the past hour. How much further?"

Isabella laughed and said, "I thought *you* were asleep for the past two hours!"

"Might have nipped a wee nap," she admitted, smiling. "It's a shame we didn't stop at the Dakhla Oasis. They have a wonderful desert lodge there," she suggested, winking at Isabella.

"Oh, I'm sorry. Did you think we would be staying at hotels on this expedition?" David leaned forward and looked over at Elsa. "We had planned to be at the dig site today, which is not within sight of any previously known archeological locations. But even though we're stopping short of our original stop, we are not close enough now not to require back-tracking to return to civilization proper. Our accommodations are tents, the men and I, but we brought the RV for Isabella, and I guess I assumed you would want to share it with her. You won't be sleeping on the ground, I assure you. We—" He paused when both Elsa and Isabella began laughing, looking back and forth between them. Realizing that Elsa had been teasing, he joined their laughter and said, "That's a relief. I envisioned calling the boss to explain why we were turning around and adding another day to our travel time."

"Elsa enjoys practical jokes, but you will discover that she's actually a very good asset on such excursions. She has an uncanny ability to locate and disarm traps and theft deterrents in ancient tombs and I am convinced the site we are seeking may be the tomb of a lesser-known priest of Isis, buried with great honor but at the location of his birthplace rather than alongside his masters in the Valley of the Kings. The chalice we seek was used by him, exclusively, in the service of his queen."

"What? This is news. What information did you discover that made you come to that conclusion, and why are you just telling me this?"

"We've Elsa to thank for most of the information," Isabella admitted. She looked out the window at the rear view mirror up ahead, next to the driver's window, and noticed the dust trail twirling around them. The vehicles behind were barely visible once the dust from the Humvee mingled with the sandy spray from the caravan. There were over a dozen transports, ranging from canvas-tarped trucks to vans and Jeeps, carrying both men and supplies. No way could they hope to slip unnoticed across the territory, she thought.

"I try to keep our database at the museum up to date," Elsa was saying. "Getting grants for digs is one of my duties, but researching them until I'm an invaluable database myself is how I manage to become crew."

"I had no idea you were such an asset, Elsa. We're lucky to have you with us," David said.

"Thanks, mate. I'm happy as a bug on any dig with Isabella, but I think I'm going to enjoy getting to know you better, too."

Isabella smiled, enjoying Elsa's obvious flirt with David. She glanced at David. His body language was warm and open, leaning toward Elsa and smiling. Perhaps he was interested in her. After all, her friend was a gorgeous redhead, single, intelligent, outgoing, sought after by many men, but though she could be precocious and flirty, she hadn't been serious about anyone since Teddy, the guy she dated for over a year before discovering he was not as honest or faithful as she'd thought. The breakup had left her friend quiet and reclusive for months. It was time for Elsa to start dating someone seriously again, Isabella decided. Why not David? He was every bit as handsome and sophisticated as Elsa had declared and an archaeologist, too. A seductive combination indeed. She could certainly understand Elsa's attraction.

"We're here."

Isabella looked out the window and realized the mounds of sand were now interspersed with clumps of vegetation, and up ahead there was a large cluster of palms and thicker vegetation, obviously circling a body of water. The oasis David had indicated. Somewhere to bathe and go for a refreshing swim, she thought. It was sure to ease the travel stiffness and lingering tension from last night's trauma. She glanced again in the driver's rear view mirror and watched the train of vehicles curve behind them, making the turn off the last hill toward the oasis. A stream of dust rose in the air far behind them, and she wondered who else could be traveling this far from civilization. But then the vehicle stopped and she reached to open the door, more concerned with stretching her legs and finding where the temporary facilities would be set up.

CHAPTER SIX

T hey're camping exactly where you predicted, Moto."

"Nowhere else for miles," Moto pointed out.

"True. Glad we brought the horses," Mukhtar said, taking Antar's reins and nodding his thanks to the teenaged boy who had led his prince's prancing black stallion over to him. "It's the only way to keep from throwing up a dust storm to alert them to our presence. Even if they've seen us in the distance, the government disguise to the vehicles should keep them from worrying about us, since we passed right past their location and kept going until they could no longer see our trail in the air behind us."

Raising his hand in the air to signal the dozen riders on the other side of the compound, Moto said, "We're ready whenever you are, My Prince."

Stepping a foot into the stirrup, Mukhtar mounted. Adar shook his head and danced by way of greeting, snorting his impatience to be off. "It seems we are ready now," he said. He leaned forward and whispered into Adar's ear. The black stallion, given his master's permission, bolted in the direction of Isabella's camp. Mukhtar leaned forward and laughed his approval.

***

"Surround the camp and keep an eye on their sentries. I'm going to the oasis and see that the crocodiles our neighbor Muhammad likes to stock his watering holes with to ward off trespassers don't welcome one of the ladies I am sure will be down to bathe," Mukhtar said.

"He won't like you killing off his guard crocs," Moto said, chuckling.

"Be sure he's compensated for that as well as the safe passage we secured for our lady's convoy."

Running down the embankment, mindful of his proximity to the camp and keeping to the lee side of the increased plant life, Mukhtar made his way to the water's edge. As he had anticipated, a pair of crocodiles, large and aging to perfection in the last warm rays of the desert sun adorned opposite sides of the pond. A pair of eye sockets, a snout and protruding nostrils revealed the presence of yet another. He signaled for Ahmed to circle around and take out the croc on the far bank and pulled his scimitar from the sheath strapped to his waist.

Moving forward, he eyed the croc and maneuvered his way around to the side. Pausing to take a breath and think ahead through his intent, he leapt forward, straddled the croc and grabbed the snout. The creature, startled, reacted with lightning speed, lashing his tail and thrashing his head. Before he could dart into the water where he would have the advantage, Mukhtar drove his dagger into the back of its head, thrusting until it was buried in the animal's brain. With a final quiver the croc went still. Pulling his knife out, which took more effort than the attack, he thrust it into the sand a few times to clean it, stood upright and looked across the water at Ahmed. He watched as the man performed a similar kill. Noting Mukhtar's attention, Ahmed smiled and gave him a thumbs-up.

Mukhtar nodded, then pulled a revolver with a silencer from his waistband and moved to the pond's edge. He aimed at the crocodile still submerged just below the surface. A slow pull on the trigger sent a bullet into the back of its head. Without movement, the reptilian sank from view. A vibration signaled a message from Moto. Pulling his phone out of his pocked, he read a short text. Lady Isabella, towels and robe in hand, was headed toward the oasis. Mukhtar pushed air with his hand and signaled for Ahmed to make himself scarce.

Once his man had disappeared over the rise, he took off his robe and kuffiyah, stashed them behind a palm and slipped into the water. The sun eased toward nightfall and cast orange hues across the horizon. Submerged to his nose, he waited for Lady Isabella to emerge from the dense growth to his left and watched with interest as she glanced around, then set a bundle of towels and clothing on the beach and began to disrobe.

Her gun belt was first and he noticed with approval the way she pulled the revolver from the holster and laid it on top of her towel, within easy reach. She bent to unlace her ankle boots and he admired the taunt curve of her buttocks, firm and rounded, as she concentrated on her task. Too soon, she stood and toed off her boots, then reached to jerk her socks off and stuff them inside. Next came her shirt, a serviceable khaki button-down, with multiple pockets and air vents across the back and under the arms. Its removal revealed a teal bra with lace across the mound of each breast. He was glad for the cool water as she stepped out of her khaki pants to reveal a skimpy pair of teal panties. She was more fully clothed than many western women at the resort pools, but he couldn't remember one that filled her bikini out nearly as well, or as enticingly.

With a final look around, she reached down and dug around in a small bag, pulling something out and shoving it into an already full bra cup, and then reached into the bag and pulled out a bottle, shaking and squeezing something into her hand. Moving to the water, she stuck a foot in, testing the temperature. Seemingly satisfied, she stepped forward, slowly, until she was midriff-high and then bent backward to submerge her hair. Rising up, she rubbed her hands together, then worked shampoo into her hair until she had produced a rich lather. Several more dips and she had removed the last of the suds. She moved back toward the shore, to shallower water, and pulled a small bottle from her bra and filled her hand again, this time with some form of body wash. He caught a whiff of oranges, clean and invigorating, and realized with a start that he had been swimming toward her, without conscious thought, drawn to her charms like a seaman to a siren, ready and willing to help her lather her silky limbs. He stilled, surprised further when his feet were able to touch the sandy bottom. How had he gotten so close?

Finished with her lathering, she turned and dove into the water, disappearing from view. He looked around, stepping backward, readying his submersion to avoid detection. *Where is she?* he wondered.

Suddenly she rose to the surface, gasped and wiped water from her eyes. She didn't at first see him, but it was far too late to avoid her. A quick blink and shock registered on her face. "You!" Her head went under water as she tried to stand and discovered the water was deeper than her height. She came back up, sputtering and choking, "What the hell?" she managed coughs and dog paddles. Without further comment she spun around and with clean strokes began power-swimming back toward shore.

Back toward help and revelation without explanation, he realized, in pursuit with a quick kickoff. When he caught her, he reached to encircle her waist and pulled her as he stood. Breathless, she struggled against him. "Are you mad?" she cried out. "Let me go this instant!"

"I am trying to protect you!" he declared, releasing her waist when she stopped struggling.

"Protect me? By sneaking up on me and grabbing me while I'm bathing?" She stood, the water reaching her midriff. Pushing her hair from her face, she glanced at his naked chest, her own still undulating with each sharp intake of breath from her exertion and emotion, then away, then back into his eyes before she stepped back a step. "What are you protecting me from?" she demanded, crossing her hands across her chest.

"From your own recklessness. Where is your escort? Why would they allow you to come down here unattended?"

"Do you suppose I need an escort to bathe?"

"Unless you do it at the bottom of the pool, or in the belly of one of those," he said, pointing to the shore. "Or that one there," he added pointing to the other shore. "And I just killed one in the middle of the pool, too," he said.

"Oh my god," she said, her hand going to her mouth. She looked around herself, backing toward shore. "Are there more?"

"It's unlikely. You're safe now, but your security team should have scouted the oasis before just letting you come down here. Do you still think you don't need my particular expertise and protection on your excursion?"

"I-it-I-it wasn't my decision. My employer refused your offer."

"And you?" he asked, moving forward, drawn once again to the pleasant citrus scent and delightful curves, to the beautiful oval-shaped face haloed even while damp with the most fascinating shade of golden hair. She had such flawless porcelain skin and amazingly expressive green eyes, presently looking up at him intently. "You have no reason to fear me. Not ever. Your safety is of great concern. Did I not prove that at your shop the other night? My business interests have not changed either, and your success on this mission is essential to them," he reminded her.

"Yes. I owe you my thanks again, it seems."

"A pleasure, My Lady," he said, smiling.

"It seems clear you would be an asset, but that doesn't change the fact that the man paying for this expedition doesn't seem to want you with us."

"So you keep repeating." He reached out to cup her shoulders in his hands, rubbing her upper arms when she shuddered in response, wondering if she felt the chemistry charge between them as strongly as he. "And what do you want, Isabella?"

Her lips, full and sensual, parted as she drew air. Sheer willpower kept his attention focused on her face rather than the seductive curve of her rising chest. But he had only so much control and she challenged it beyond reason. Leaning down, he captured her lips with his own, gently and tentatively at first, but when she responded rather than pulling away, he drew her closer, slipping his right hand behind her back to press her against him, deepening the kiss. She parted her lips and allowed his tongue to explore and tease, coaxing hers to dance in the age-old rhythm of passion and intoxicating desire.

Isabella knew she should pull away, should force herself to resist the primal attraction she had felt for him since the moment he'd walked into her shop. But if she'd thought him an attractive man when fully clothed, this new, closer, half-naked male specimen was beyond her current ability to withstand. It took more than horseback riding to get abs like that and his chest, broad and softly-furred, expanded to well-honed arms and shoulders strong enough to hold an entire kingdom, one that he would someday command, she reminded herself. But then she lost her thought-thread, melting against the warmth of his body as he pulled her damp flesh closer, chilled from the cool water and adrenaline dissipation.

The man's pheromones were addictive. She closed her eyes and leaned into him, letting him lead her on a magical moment of sheer emotional and physical decadence. His tongue seduced her senses, coaxing her into willing surrender. Tingles of heat flooded to the join of her legs and an aching need burned within her. What was wrong with her? She wasn't this kind of woman. She wanted him, a virtual stranger, to take her right here and now, to ravish her in a desert oasis filled with crocodiles. The danger involved was beyond reason, on so many levels. She groaned softly, reaching up to wrap her fingers in his shoulder-length hair and clasp the back of his neck, wanting him closer, wanting him inside her.

He responded to her urging and pressed his loins against her. Instead of feeling shock at the evidence of his desire, she moved to accommodate him and wrapped her legs around him eagerly as he reached to scoop her buttocks and lift her up to meet him.

"Isabella? You still down here? Are you okay?"

He lifted his head and she tried to bring his lips, his tongue, his attention back to her, pulling at the back of his head. "Your friend, Elsa," he whispered.

"Isabella? Where are you?"

He lowered her, letting her feet return to the sand, her sanity to the moment.

"Isa--"

"I'm here," she called. She pushed against his chest, for leverage and mental stability. *What should I say?* she wondered, confused and still breathless from his torrid kisses. She'd never been kissed that way before, not by anyone. Her undeniable attraction to him was primitive. He awoke raw desire within her until she was so lost in the feelings her brain stopped controlling her actions. The prince was dangerous, on so many levels. She could tell that he, too, was moved by their exchange. His chest rose and fell swiftly and his hand lingered on the curve of her buttock. The intensity of his stare unnerved her, eyes darkened by lust, lips parted with soft puffs of air matching the rhythmic swell of his rib cage.

Running from her own uncertainty, she turned to shore and waded quickly toward the sound of Elsa's voice.

As she reached dry sand, she ran forward and bent down to pick up her robe and shook it before putting it on. She did the same with the towel, wrapping it around her wet hair. She turned back to the prince, shivering in the breeze. He was gone. She strained to find him in the fading light, her attention moving from the water to the shoreline.

"Here you are, love! Look at you shuttering from that cold water. Should have used the shower in that big RV. I would have waited and gone last if I knew you were going to come down here and freeze your bum off. Damn cold once the sun goes down. Come on, it's time for dinner. I was beginning to think you'd been eaten by jackals," Elsa said. "David was all set to fetch you, but I reminded him you might be in the altogether. If I didn't know better, I'd say he was even more inclined to come, but I've got my own plans for that lad."

Isabella pulled on her socks and boots, not bothering with the ties, other than tucking the ends into the tops. She gathered her things, heard a soft splash to her right, and smiled slightly as she realized the prince hadn't been eaten by a croc or the splashes would have been violent and much louder. With a lookout for crocs, she tagged along beside Elsa on the way back to camp, letting her talkative friend carry on her side of the conversation as she tried to process all that had just happened.

Prince Mukhtar would be a huge asset, which he had proved more than once now, but she wasn't sure he was good for her emotional wellbeing, however safe he could keep her from dangers other than himself. He was a prince and probably already had a harem even though local gossip found it strange he didn't have a dozen wives by now. He was certainly not for her. No. She needed to steer clear of that hazard.

CHAPTER SEVEN

Isabella awoke with a start. She sat up and looked around in the dim light cast by the battery-operated floor lighting. She didn't see anything unusual, but a feeling of dread overwhelmed her. "Elsa? Elsa!"

"Hm?"

"Something's wrong. Wake up."

Elsa sat up and reached for the bedside lamp.

"No. Don't turn on the lights," she whispered.

"Why?" Elsa asked, adopting her low tone and sense of urgency.

"Shhh. I don't know what, but something isn't right. I heard something."

"What did you hear?"

"I'm not sure. It woke me."

Isabella reached down and grabbed her robe from the end of the bed. She put it on, got out of bed and felt around for her slippers. Scuffing them on, she cautiously moved toward the doorway. Elsa stood up and followed her, shoving her arms into her own robe. Isabella turned and held her finger to her lips, signaling her to keep quiet.

They moved down the short walkway, past the bathroom and then the furnace and water heater and storage closet doors and into the main seating and kitchen area of the RV. Suddenly there was a thud against the side of the vehicle. They both spun around, toward the bedroom and the area from which the sound had originated. Elsa grabbed hold of Isabella's arm. Neither of them spoke. Isabella disengaged herself from Elsa and stepped toward the pedestal table that was bolted to the floor on their left. She reached to pull her revolver from the holster she had left on the bench seat. Pointing it toward the floor, she pulled back the hammer, set the holster on the table and kneeled on the bench, inching her way toward the window. There was a small gap between the blinds and she pressed closer, trying to see toward the back of the RV.

She saw shadows, varying shades of darkness.

"Can you see anything?" Elsa whispered from behind her.

She shook her head negatively.

Thunk. Then a scraping sound, followed by another bang. This time on the opposite side of the motor home, directly across from them, behind the stove and sink in the kitchenette. Dishes rattled in the cupboards with the force of the next blows from outside.

"Shit," Elsa said softly, stepping aside to let Isabella shuffle out of the narrow space between the table and the bench back. She stood and turned toward the exterior door to the left of the kitchenette, raised her revolver and waiting for whoever was outside the RV to attempt entry.

Several quiet but tense moments later, Elsa whispered, "Maybe they left?"

"If that were the case, wouldn't David or one of the men come to check on us?"

"If they could," Elsa said softly, giving voice to Isabella's thoughts that something might have happened to them.

She and Elsa would have to defend themselves, she decided. Turning back to the table, she pulled her backpack off the opposite seat, slowly unzipped the rear pocket to avoid making any sound, and pulled out her sheathed scimitar. "Here," she told Elsa, who nodded, pulling the dagger from its leather home.

"There's not another gun?" Elsa inquired.

Isabella paused, trying to remember if she had put the semi-automatic in the overhead or the supply van. She reached up and opened the cupboard above the table, feeling a sense of relief when she saw the assault rifle. Grasping it by the barrel, she pulled it down. Elsa quickly put the dagger on the table and reached for the gun, expertly dropping a bullet into the chamber and preparing the weapon for firing.

A firm knocking sounded on the door. Both women swiveled toward the door, aiming. "Who is it?" Isabella asked.

"It's me, David. Are you okay?"

Isabella let her breath out in a sigh of relief.

"Thank God," Elsa said. She walked to the door and flipped the switch that lit an exterior light above the door, then pulled back the blind. Apparently satisfied that the person outside was indeed David, she unlocked the door and pushed it open, lowering the steps. "Are we ever glad to see you," she said, moving back and pointing the gun toward the floor.

"What happened?" Isabella asked as David stepped into the trailer.

"Desertion."

"What? But what was all that noise? Someone was bumping into the sides of the RV. It sounded like fighting or someone struggling."

"That was the head of security, trying to prevent some of his men from leaving because they were stealing equipment. They did manage to get two vehicles, but he prevented them from taking the supply van."

"Why were they leaving now?" Elsa asked.

"It appears that they joined the crew with the intention of stealing some of our most expensive technology."

"You must be joking. What all did they get?" Isabella asked, setting her gun on the table.

David glanced at it, and then at the rifle in Elsa's hand and chuckled. "I guess I didn't need to worry about you ladies, after all."

"Well, we are both pretty good shots," Isabella said.

"Good. Sahib is doing an inventory with his veteran soldiers. The ones that were trying to steal from us were additional men who had been hired by our employer and not me, ironically. He's not going to be very happy to hear about what happened," David said.

"I bet not, but at least he can't blame you," Isabella pointed out. "We need to see what they got away with. Let us get dressed. We would have been waking up in a half-hour anyway."

"Of course. I'm just glad the two of you are unharmed. We think they were planning to break into the RV and take whatever communication or sensory equipment they could get. They knew we stored some of it in here. As it turns out, it's a good thing we did. I put the imaging equipment in the forward cupboards myself. We would have had to wait for replacements in order to get started at the dig site."

"You really think they were trying to break in here?" Elsa asked, glancing at Isabella, her drawn brows and frown conveying her worry.

"Sahib and one of his men got into a confrontation with two of them right outside, which is probably why you heard anything at all. The cowards ran away, so rest assured they will not be back."

"There, you see, Elsa? We are perfectly safe now, and Sahib and his men are very good at what they do because they stopped the men before they were able to complete their robbery."

Elsa nodded, then shrugged, clearly not yet convinced.

"I'll let you ladies get dressed then, and have cook get breakfast going." He pointed to the pod coffee machine on the countertop and said, "Your coffee is just a push button away. The drawer it's sitting on is fully stocked with more variety in the cup cupboard in the overhead to the right of the sink. I had some yesterday. It's pretty good."

"Perfect," Elsa said.

David flipped the overhead lights on, waved and hurried down the steps, closing the door behind him and giving the knob a rattle to be sure it was locked.

Elsa hurried toward the cupboard and pulled out a pair of coffee cups and then stepped over to the coffee machine, pulled open the drawer, grabbed a pod and started the machine. "There's tea, too, Earl Grey, thank goodness. But you probably want espresso, right?" she asked Isabella.

"That would be wonderful," Isabella said, heading back to the bedroom to get dressed.

"Hey, Isabella?"

She turned back. "Yes?"

"Aren't you even a little worried about how much danger and what near misses we have experienced before we even began the dig on this project? I think you need to try to find out who your anonymous boss is, or what exactly he wants this chalice for. These aren't coincidences and we are definitely not in the loop."

"Right there with you, Elsa. I plan to demand answers from David as soon as we find out exactly what has happened."

Her second cup of espresso in hand, Isabella walked up to David, who was in conversation with Sahib outside the supply van. "How bad is it?"

"It could have been much worse. They mainly took backup equipment, which is what was in the back of the transportation vehicles, but they still got several thousands of dollars in electronics and two Humvees. Unfortunately, they got the satellite hookup, so the boss is sending another one by helicopter. He's pretty angry."

David had turned toward her and was gazing into her eyes, intently. She knew his eyes were brown, but she didn't recall them having such a mahogany tint to them. They seemed to have golden flecks in them too, as though they were backlit by a sunset. She hadn't noticed how beautiful his eyes were before. Why not? Isabella wondered. And he smelled so good, too, like a forest back in England, after a spring rain. A new cologne evidently. "I-I'm sure you let him know it was the new men he sent, right?"

"Of course," he said softly, "he places no blame on me or any of the remaining crew."

"That's good," she said. Why was she suddenly so attracted to David?

He placed his hands on her shoulders and said, "I'm just glad you're safe, no matter what else they were able to take."

She felt so warm and protected with David, thankful he was there.

"Here you are," Elsa said, approaching.

David withdrew his hands and turned toward her best friend, and she felt a strong loss at the break in contact, and sudden anger at Elsa for taking David's attention from her. She stopped herself from snapping at her.

"And here you are," David said, smiling.

Why was she so angry to see David being friendly toward Elsa? Just a few minutes ago she had been glad about Elsa's attraction for the man, and had even encouraged her to pursuit a potential relationship with David.

The sound of vehicles approaching distracted her and they all turned to see a trio of Humvees. "Are they coming back?" Isabella asked incredulously, reaching for the revolver in her gun belt. She felt surprise as well as relief to see Sahib and his men rush forward, lifting machine guns toward the newcomers.

The small convoy stopped and several men stepped out, all wearing the signature blue garb of Prince Mukhtar's Bedouins.

Sahib fired a round into the air and shouted, "Halt!" in Arabic.

The men stopped, arms raised in the air.

"Wait," Isabella said loudly. "It's Prince Mukhtar." She walked forward, toward the prince who was wearing the gold agal that distinguished him, feeling somewhat awkward but certainly not afraid after what had passed between them last night.

"Hold on," David said, reaching out to grasp her arm and stop her. "Let's find out what our visitors want first," he added. His fingers on her bare skin reminded her of how David had made her feel a few minutes ago. Isabella turned her head and looked up into his intense stare.

"Of course, David," she said, smiling at his obvious concern for her safety and the protective stance he was taking. It felt good to have someone care so much about her.

He moved forward and walked up to the prince. They stood in conversation for a few minutes, the prince gesturing toward the vehicles. Then, to her surprise, they clasped hands and laughed. David turned, walking toward her with the prince.

"It seems the prince saw our former employees absconding with our gear and managed to stop them and retrieve our supplies. We owe him a debt and unless you object I have overridden our employer's orders in this case and agreed to let him join us. We could use the additional protection, just in case, especially now that we have lost so many men."

"No, no, I don't object. If you think it's for the best, I agree completely," Isabella said.

"I second Isabella's vote," Elsa said, walking up to stand beside her.

"I thank you for your vote of confidence, Ms . . . "

"Hopkins, but as I told you at the hotel, just call me Elsa."

"Elsa, of course. Thank you," the prince said, flashing the gorgeous smile that made Isabella's heart beat faster.

Apparently equally impressed, Elsa said, "No, thank you, Prince Mukhtar. I will sleep much better tonight knowing you and your men are looking out for us."

"Which doesn't mean that we weren't already safe with David and his men here to protect us, obviously," Isabella quickly pointed out.

"Between the two of us, you ladies have nothing further to worry about," David said. He reached to take Elsa's arm and added, "Breakfast is probably ready by now. What say we eat before it grows cold?" He turned to look at the prince and said, "You will join us, surely, Your Highness?"

Isabella managed to take her attention from where David's hand rested on Elsa's elbow and looked at Mukhtar.

"You are most kind. I would be delighted, Mr. Khourey." The prince wasn't looking at David when he answered. He was staring straight at her as though recalling their evening adventure . . . or perhaps he was wondering if she was remembering, and was gauging her reaction to his presence. *What is it about Prince Mukhtar and his sudden appearances?* she wondered.

"David, please, Your Highness. Call me David."

"Mukhtar, then. Thank you, David."

CHAPTER EIGHT

They still tailing us?"

Moto pointed to the screen on his notebook and said, "Right there. Just far enough out to keep us from seeing any dust they're kicking up. We should have scanned her vehicles. They probably planted a tracker."

"We need to find out who they are. And I still don't get how Set's man, David, allowed some other faction to infiltrate his group," Mukhtar said.

"Or why he would go to so much trouble to make Lady Isabella think it was a robbery gone bad."

"Well that part I get—the same reason we told her we had taken the men to the police rather than sending them to Ljluka for questioning. It will all be clearer once Ljluka's men find out who's tailing us."

"Looks like we're there," Moto said.

Mukhtar looked out the window and watched as Ahmed pulled the Land Rover up alongside the Humvee in which Lady Isabella, Elsa and David were traveling. He saw nothing but open desert for miles around, one sand dune looking much the same as the next, varying shades of tan-hued sienna ripples caused by windblown sands and looking off in the distance like rusty water moved by a gentle breeze. It didn't surprise him though. Dig sites often originated in open desert. As the sand removal progressed the buried architecture quickly emerged.

He opened his door and unfolded his long legs before he stepped from the vehicle and stretched to kick-start his circulation. Lady Isabella descended from her vehicle with the aid of the running board and much to his enjoyment she bent down to touch her toes, then raised up, hands over her head and bent one way, then the other, as tired of car-riding as he, apparently.

He paused as David approached around the front of the Land Rover. "Just a quick word, Mukhtar, if you don't mind."

"Of course."

"There's no need to worry the ladies needlessly. I wouldn't like for you to mention our fan club back there, at least not for now. My boss is looking into it."

"Fan club?"

David chuckled. "Okay, have it your way, my friend. Thanks for your discretion."

Mukhtar smiled without commitment and continued toward Lady Isabella. She was digging in the back of the vehicle and stood up hauling a backpack onto her shoulder. Elsa came around the vehicle and waved when she saw Mukhtar.

"You look none the worse for our morning drive," he said.

"That's a huge compliment indeed," Elsa said. "I'm just glad we're finally here. And right up there," she gestured to her right, up in front of their vehicles, "is where we will start digging." She turned toward Isabella and pointed to her computer screen. We should have the crew start digging here while we have lunch. By the time we're done, if this map is correct, and I agree with you that it is, they should have found the outer structure."

"An excellent idea," David said. "We can set up the perimeter ropes while cook prepares lunch and get started. We should be well under way before dark."

Mukhtar felt a surge of adrenaline. He loved the discovery of a new archeological site and this one was no exception. "Just set me to work, Lady Isabella. My men and I are at your disposal."

"Wonderful. It's going to go so much faster with more crew who are experienced at dig sites as you informed us yours are," she said, clearly as excited as he was at the prospect of getting started. Her eyes were shining, her cheeks slightly flushed, and she was talking much faster than usual for her, though still not as fast as her friend, Elsa, who he sometimes had to ask to repeat what she had said so he could catch it."

They walked toward the front of the vehicles, where the men had already begun lining up supplies, including a now open case of wooden stakes and bundles of rope. Isabella sat her backpack on the ground and began walking away from it with Elsa, both their heads bent over Elsa's notebook. When they had walked about thirty paces away, they stopped and turned back.

"My backpack and here are the two northern markers," she called back loudly.

Mukhtar grabbed a stake, sledge hammer and some rope and motioned for Moto to do the same. His crew quickly followed, grabbing stakes and hurrying after him to space out some supports along the rope line.

In just under an hour they had staked out the perimeter and the area Isabella wanted digging to begin. Mukhtar provided the large canvas tarp for them to erect over the area of heavy lifting to shield it from the unrelenting midday sun. He also provided strips of processed wood that trailed across the sand to allow easier cart rolling for the men. The crew was soon at work shoveling wheelbarrows of sand and taking turns redepositing it a ways from the dig site along the wooden path.

"You really have been on dig sites before, haven't you?" Lady Isabella said as they walked toward the air-conditioned comfort of the RV.

"You doubted me?" Mukhtar said, laughing down at her.

She grinned and shrugged. "I can't believe my crew didn't pack any tarps to use as sunshades, or even planking for the sand removal."

Mukhtar glanced over toward David and Elsa, bent over her computer and pointing to various locations within the dig perimeter. "I'm surprised David didn't have them included in his order supply, but perhaps they were omitted by the suppliers who were scrambling to fill the order on such short notice. No matter. I'm glad I was able to help."

"You are always helping, showing up at just the right moment, with just what is needed," Isabella said gratefully, but he saw something else flicker in her eyes. Suspicion?

"I have attempted to do all in my power to make you safe and keep this mission on schedule," he said.

"Ah yes, the artifact. David has agreed to let you have a photo of the artifact. You must surely be pleased."

"Of course. That was ever my goal."

"You have more than earned it," she said, and this time she seemed completely sincere.

They reached the RV and the stairs lowered to allow her to enter. Even from a distance he could feel the cool air of the interior and hurried after her. Though he was well used to the desert heat, he didn't object to a midday cool off. At night, however, he preferred the tents his men had erected, cooled by the chill desert breezes at night and furnished with Persian carpeting, soft couches and pillows, drapes of silken fabrics and soft animal fur throws. He looked forward to introducing Isabella to the luxuries of a true Bedouin's tent, a virtual palace once made only from goatskins and beautiful, hand-woven fabrics. With the advent of much lighter, high-tech fabrics, many of the Bedouin customs were changing, but he'd been raised in tents and despite owning several large mansions, his family still preferred the mobility.

"Oh, it smells delicious," Isabella said. "I didn't realize how hungry I was."

The door opened and Elsa entered, followed by David. "I think they're going to find the entrance today," she said to Isabella. "I can't believe how fast that crew is moving. We've never had such a skilled crew before. This is certainly not their first dig and they work together as if they'd been a team forever, instead of two crews thrown together at the last moment."

"I have a feeling," Isabella said, "that Prince Mukhtar's men are well used to flexibility in the face of diverse situations."

"Wonderful work qualities, you must admit," he said.

"True. Not easily achieved with such a large group. But then this is only a fraction of the force at your disposal, isn't it?" David inquired.

Mukhtar looked at David, realizing the man seldom said anything that didn't have an underlying meaning as well. What, he wondered, was the man trying to discover? "I have more men, yes. I didn't feel it necessary to bring more on this mission. Too many and they begin to get in each other's way."

"Yes, yes you wouldn't want them to do that. They seem to be working well with my crew, too, and this is not the crew I usually procure. They were unavailable on such short notice. That is also, unfortunately, why we had a problem with the last-minute men our boss provided."

"Yes, it is difficult to find good help," Mukhtar agreed, meeting David's gaze steadily as he delivered an underlying message of his own.

"Oh, let's eat. That smells so good. I'm starving."

Lady Isabella laughed, seemingly unaware of the male posturing, and said, "I just said much the same thing."

The women scooted into the interior of the booth seating and the men sat down across from each other. The banter remained civilized and focused on the dig, the possibility of finding the relic, and what period and possible theft deterrents they were likely to encounter.

Whatever else David may have had to scrimp on, the cook wasn't one of them. Their luncheon as predicted was delicious, thin savory slices of goat meat served with hot flat bread, olives and fresh diced greens, cilantro, parsley, tomatoes and sesame seeds, drizzled with olive oil and lemon juice. They washed it down with mint tea, and were soon out the door and on their way back to the dig.

Approaching the top of the hill that had been formed by the progressive digging, they saw Moto running toward them.

As they moved closer they were able to make out what he was saying. "They found it," Moto yelled, waving his arm back toward the bottom of the widening trench to hurry their descent. "They found it!"

CHAPTER NINE

Isabella broke into a run and rushed toward Moto. "The entrance? They found the entrance?"

"Yes, yes," Moto said, excitement obvious in his voice and body language as he pointed toward the awning behind him.

They hurried down the incline that had been created by the excavation, stopping as they reached the bottom of the hill where the sand gave way to a stone wall. The wall, about a foot of it visible, revealed the upper curves of carved sculptures and ancient hieroglyphics. "You were right," Elsa said.

"So far the map has been right," Isabella pointed out. "If the doorway is here, facing this direction, it may even be the right tomb," she said. "I need my tools!" Turning, she nearly collided with David, laughed and said, "Sorry. I have to get my tools."

She hated to be too optimistic. She'd been disappointed on digs before and this one seemed to be progressing too fast and too well to be true, but Isabella couldn't deny that her breathlessness was from more than the jog back up the hill. The archaeologist in her couldn't wait to get sand under her nails and in her hair wherever it inevitably escaped the confines of her braid and elastic ties and dragged across whatever piece of ancient stone or relic she was working on. Picking up her pace, she raced toward the supply van.

She spotted her bright neon-yellow tool box, dirty and dented from years of field work, but still sturdy and functional. Grabbing the black rubber handle, she hefted it from the truck and shouldered the double doors closed, then hurried back toward the dig site and the strangest crew she'd ever had on an excavation.

She'd still found no answers to the real questions she had about the artifact and David insisted he knew nothing more than she did about the purpose of the relic or who their employer was beyond a phone number. She believed him, too, he was so sincere and genuinely concerned about her welfare and success.

Mukhtar was another issue.

Despite their obvious physical attraction, she wasn't at all sure she could trust him. Even if his men were following her in an attempt to keep her safe, which he would probably never admit to, that didn't explain how he had known she was being threatened by robbers, twice, and crocodiles, crocodiles for god's sake. He had finally convinced even David that they needed his help. But what if he was the one who had someone break into her shop just so he could rush in and save her? What if the technology thieves actually worked for him too? They had no proof he had taken them to the police instead of sending them home after a job well done. Same with the thieves in her shop. That would explain why *fake* policemen took them away so quickly. There were the crocs though. There was no denying he might well have saved her from being on the menu.

She lugged her toolbox to the planks and wasn't disappointed when one of Mukhtar's men insisted on taking it from her, with an, "You should have told us you were fetching something so heavy, Lady Isabella. One of us would have been happy to come along and assist you."

She smiled her thanks while harboring a nagging wonder at the overly solicitous and almost unbelievable way in which Mukhtar and his men had ingratiated themselves and once given entry had practically taken over, all the while attending to her every want or need so that no fault could be found. *Clever,* she thought. *Very clever.*

"Isabella, why didn't you ask for help," David said as she approached.

"It's fine. I always drag that thing around," she said, returning his smile, glad that she could at least trust David's sincerity.

"They've uncovered the threshold," Mukhtar said. "There's a warning, a curse. I think we're in the right place."

Isabella glanced at him in surprise. *He can read ancient hieroglyphics?* He was obviously experienced and now knowledgeable. Maybe he really did need a symbol on the back of the chalice. But what if that was the reason her boss wanted it too? What if they were handing her boss's rival the key to an even greater treasure? She needed to speak to David about it, sooner rather than later.

But for now, she hurried forward, kneeled in front of the uncovered wall and threw open her toolbox, pulling out what most laymen would view as an oversized wallpaper brush. She wasn't smoothing on paste, however, she was delicately removing sand and dirt from the time-worn surface of a tomb threshold she expected to be over two-thousand years old.

She glanced over to see Mukhtar who was engaged in a similar activity several feet down the wall, uncovering the face of a statue that ironically looked to have the head of a crocodile, the god of art and creativity. Elsa knelt down beside her. "Hand me a brush," she said. "I'll help you with the threshold so we can read it and hopefully discover who, and therefore what, may be in here."

Isabella reached into her toolbox and handed a thickly-bristled brush about an inch shorter than hers to Elsa. Together, starting at opposite sides, they cleared the upper threshold. David, she noticed with appreciation, was overseeing the broadening and continued sand removal from the narrow ramp that led to the entrance.

Isabella reached into her pocket and pulled out her phone. Snapping a few pictures, she glanced at Elsa who was already looking at her and grinning. Together they said softly, "It's him."

"What did you say? Is it the tomb we seek?" David asked from behind them where he had obviously been watching their progress with interest.

"Yes!" Isabella said, jumping up and turning to face him. "Look there," she said, pointing toward the hieroglyphics. "It says, *cursed be all who enter here. May they die a thousand deaths and may Anubis find their heart hollow and filled with evil deeds and the greed befitting those who would disrupt the eternal home of Ishmael, son of Mumbai the great, holy priest of Isis, mother goddess and fearful protector of those who would cause harm to her beloved children, those who pay homage to her unrivaled beauty and omniscient power.*"

"Wonderful," David said. He gazed into her eyes and she could see how pleased he was, the golden flecks in his eyes seemed almost to dance with joy. When he reached out to give her an exuberant hug, she responded, feeling as though actual sparks passed between them. They both laughed with happiness.

"It's Ismael." Mukhtar said from behind her, his inflection sounding as if he already knew the answer.

She separated from David, feeling suddenly self-conscious.

"It's him," she affirmed, realizing that Mukhtar had probably read the curse and actually knew as much as she did.

"Wonderful. Let's allow the crew to finish clearing a path to the door. They have a good momentum going and if we get out of their way they may have it cleared before dark."

"Excellent suggestion, Prince Mukhtar. That will give us time to study some ancient writings I was able to obtain copies of regarding this secretive priest of Isis. It may help us in defusing any theft deterrents these wily ancients came up with."

"Can't hurt," Elsa said, brushing sand from her backside. "This cult was particularly diabolical in their attempts to protect their gateways to the afterlife."

"Something I'm not likely to forget," Isabella said softly.

Elsa gave her a quick hug. "Don't worry, love. I won't let what happened to your father happen to you. I'll make sure we find all the traps. I promise."

Isabella smiled sadly. "I know you will, Elsa. You help me keep a cool head so I don't rush forward without caution, too, my father's fatal flaw." She noticed Mukhtar staring at her oddly, as though he'd overheard, and quickly turned away to stow her tools in their carrying case. He made her feel vulnerable, and it wasn't an emotion with which she was comfortable.

Clustered around the bench table, Isabella finished reading the document and passed it to Mukhtar, who, she was strangely jealous to admit, read it much more quickly than she had. "It appears he was a high priest, devoted to Isis and acting as an intermediary, bringing her messages directly to the people.

"A sayer then? Like an oracle?" Elsa asked.

"According to this historic rendering, he was not psychic or even intuitive, in the usual sense of oracle. It doesn't talk about him as though he saw visions or had dreams, but as though he literally spoke to Isis and she answered. More like a telepath, with her able to read his mind and place her thoughts in his head so that he understood what she wanted. He wasn't in an altered state such as a trance or sleep," Isabella explained.

"So they literally believed Isis was with them, a goddess who could walk among them and interact with them," Elsa said.

"Of course," David and Mukhtar said together, then looked at each other and chuckled.

Isabella glanced between them. Their tone had been more than affirmative. It sounded as though they too believed Isis was a very real, literal entity and were surprised at Elsa's questioning of that fact.

Rumors sometimes tied Prince Mukhtar to the Illuminati, a secret cult known to exist since at least the time of the Pharaohs who built the pyramids. Until this moment, she had always dismissed those rumors as passed along by those wishing to cast even more mystique on the infamous persona of one of the country's wealthiest and certainly most eligible bachelors. The Illuminati itself was an organization which, though it had certainly existed since she herself had seen ancient artifacts whose writings and symbolisms supported its existence in Egypt, was unable to be tied to any one deity, purpose or era. Illuminati was a word most often whispered with respect, almost reverence, among the superstitious Egyptians, as though it still existed and was to be feared. *Could those rumors be true? What might it have to do with this artifact they sought?*

***

"Lady Isabella? Do you wish the men to remove the outer stone to the tomb?"

"What? Oh, yes, of course,"

"Then we need to step back and let them have access," Mukhtar said.

"Of course." Isabella turned and stooped to pack her tools back into her utility box and snapped the lid closed. When Mukhtar reached for it, she said, "Thank you," and followed Elsa up the hill.

"How long do you think it'll take?" Elsa was asking David.

"An hour perhaps, so you'll still have a few hours of daylight." David's smile included Isabella as he looked toward her.

"Wonderful," Isabella said. "David, may I speak to you privately for a moment?"

"Let's go to the RV," he suggested.

She nodded and led the way. It was time to speak to David about her suspicions regarding Mukhtar.

Once they reached the vehicle, she hurried up the steps and took a seat at the table. David sat across from her and said, "Is anything wrong?" He leaned forward and clasped her hand. "You're worried about something. Please, you know you can tell me anything. What can I do to help?"

His eyes were so warm and encouraging. He exuded sincerity and concern. She's had such a hard time trusting anyone since her father left her feeling abandoned and desolate, with no one but distant relatives in England since her grandparents passed. And she knew they disapproved of her, those left since her only aunt had passed away last year. They thought her indulgent father had raised her like a wild native except for the even lonelier times she'd been forced to attend boarding school in a wet, frigid country that never felt like home to her. But now here was David, whose honesty and unconditional concern for her reminded her of her father, though even her father hadn't given her so much undivided attention. Was David in love with her? But wait, he was for Elsa and she's been with . . .

"Name it, and if it is in my power, I will grant it to you," David said, smiling.

"I'm not sure. I mean, what's your take on Prince Mukhtar?"

He sat up, clearly surprised by her sudden inquiry. "A wonderful asset to both our security and archaeology teams. What exactly are you asking me?"

"Yes, but he's almost too helpful. Do you trust him?"

"Trust him?" His brows furrowed and he glanced toward the window that faced the dig site. "I've no reason *not* to trust him. Do you know something that I don't? Do *you* trust him?"

"Yes, of course. I mean, well, I'm not sure. It's just that he seems almost too good to be true, always there whenever I—I mean we, need him most."

"He does play a guardian angel rather well." David chuckled. "You're just not used to being looked after. I suspect your longstanding sense of independence is irked at accepting help from anyone. That and trust just isn't in your comfort zone."

"Well, I--"

"No, I get it. I really do, Isabella. I lost my own parents at a young age and that fear of abandonment prevented me from being able to trust people for a really long time."

Isabella hesitated. Was that it? Did his constant rescues make her feel incapable of taking care of herself? Did she somehow resent his interferences, even if they were made with the best of intentions and even if they saved her life? She had to admit that she hadn't had more than a casual business dinner with a man in a very long time. David made her sound like she had some serious control issues.

"You must be right, David. Mukhtar has been nothing but cooperative and helpful."

"Good. It's settled then. We'll give him the benefit of the doubt, and just to be on the safe side, I'll still keep my eyes open. But I don't want you to worry about it. You've been through enough. Just focus on getting the artifact. Deal?"

"Deal," Isabella said, and she looked deep into his eyes. His gaze was steady and sure, reassuring. She realized how foolish she had been to worry about anything but the relic. That's all that mattered. David would take care of everything else. Mukhtar and David only wanted to help her find the artifact.

CHAPTER TEN

et? It can't be. Why would he do that? Are you sure? So now we have to watch out for all of them," Mukhtar said. He pressed the end button on his phone and looked across the table at Moto.

"What has Set done now?"

"His men are the ones who have been following us."

"So who does David work for then?"

"That's the big question. It settles some questions and creates more. I was wondering how it was possible that I genuinely liked David if he was one of Set's men. They're usually so arrogant and controlling. David may actually be exactly who he says he is, because his identity and backstory check out, but that begs the question of who has actually hired Lady Isabella to find the artifact and what do they want it for."

"Could it actually be a collector?"

"Doubtful."

"Someone who wants to sell it back to us?"

"Suicide, and thus also doubtful."

"And we're sure he's not working for Set?"

"Ljluka thinks he may actually have killed Set's men. Those men we turned over to him?"

"Yeah?"

"They weren't thieves, trying to get away with merchandise. They were fleeing, and there were a lot more of them, almost a dozen men who according to the survivors were murdered by David."

"So where are the bodies and why would David make up such an elaborate lie for Lady Isabella."

"Bodies are easy to dispose of in the desert. Perhaps he was trying to protect her? He seems overly solicitous toward her. Didn't want to scare her or Elsa? The bigger question is," Prince Mukhtar said, "why did he just go along with our story of turning the thieves over to the authorities?"

"Yes," Moto said, nodding. "You would think he would be worried they'd tell us the truth."

"Which means he doesn't care if the men who got away told us the truth, and he's purposely keeping us close to him."

"He may plan to kill us as well. He has around fifteen men, so we clearly have him outnumbered. Do you suppose he wants us to help protect them from Set? He has to know Set would just send more men, even if he removed them from his party. Do you think any of his men are still working for Set?"

Mukhtar stood and walked over and looked out of the window blind on the door. Seeing Isabella and David emerge from her RV, he said, "We need to get back out there. Just keep all the men on high alert. There is much more to David than is obvious, that's for certain. It's best to view them all as potential threats to our mission."

Walking up to Lady Isabella, Mukhtar said, "So they've reached the door. Do you think it's rigged?"

"It's a good possibility. Elsa and I were just about to examine the edges for anything obvious, but there's seldom anything obvious about the hidden security in these tombs."

"True," Mukhtar said, moving toward the entrance with Isabella.

"I can't find anything," Elsa said, turning from the entryway where she'd been dusting the edges of the door with a stiff paint brush.

Isabella stepped to the doorway and bent to run her fingers along the edge, where the stone slab that served as a door met the threshold. Elsa followed suit on the opposite side.   Mukhtar raised his hand to signal Moto, who called out to one of his men. Soon a man was running down the hill to bring them a short stepladder. Mukhtar nodded his thanks and set it in front of the doorway and climbed to the top, running his fingers across the indentation across the top.

"I found something," he said. "Step back, ladies."

Isabella and Elsa dutifully hurried back a few steps and watched as Mukhtar pressed the symbol of the bird near the top of the door. It moved inward a few inches, a click sounded and then he jumped down, grabbed the ladder and stepped back himself. A heavy grating, the sound of sand rubbing between large stones signaled a shift in the door's position. A rope pulley system activated somewhere within the interior and shifting sand could be heard funneling away as the door slid open, the stone slipping into a crevice behind the threshold on the left. The mechanism worked exactly as the immortal, adopted son of Isis, Prince Ljluka, had instructed him earlier.

"How the hell did you find that?" Isabella said softly.

"I felt the slight indentation around the symbol on the upper edge," Mukhtar said, shrugging and grinning down at her. She was clearly excited, her eyes wide and shiny.

"David, do you have the torches?" she called, turning toward David who was hurrying down the incline toward her. He was followed by two other men, all of whom were carrying both butane lanterns and battery operated torches.

"Yes, here," he said, handing her a high-beam halogen torch. More torches were distributed to Elsa and Mukhtar.

Switching them on, the group turned to Isabella expectantly.

"Well, let's see how far we can get," she said, entering the dark tunnel revealed by the now open stone door. Elsa was elbow to elbow, with Mukhtar and David close behind.

Knowing what was ahead, Mukhtar watched her carefully. Making sure she remained safe while not revealing his prior knowledge of the tomb's deterrents would be tricky.

She shone her beam across the side of the passageway, then down the other side. When she revealed some hieroglyphics on the wall to her left she stopped and shone her light on the ceiling, then the floor.

"Do you need an air hose?" Mukhtar asked.

"Yes, yes that would be best," she murmured, moving closer to the pictures and ancient writing on the hall's wall.

Mukhtar pulled out his phone but discovered zero bars. He lifted it and Moto said, "I'll go," and turned to run out of the tomb.

"He's handy, isn't he?" David said softly.

Mukhtar looked at him sharply, trying to gauge the truth behind his innocent inquiry from his facial expression, as much as it was visible in the cone of torch light thrown against the wall behind him.

"Invaluable," Mukhtar agreed. David had already returned his attention to Isabella and her examination of the writings on the wall. His face was hungry and the morphology Mukhtar witnessed he recognized. David wasn't just excited to discover the artifact, he was desperate, as eager as an opium addict packing a pipe. For the first time, Mukhtar felt alarm. Every instinct he had told him something about David wasn't right.

"What does it say?" David asked eagerly.

"Most of this is just more threats against tomb raiders, and endless accolades for the priest buried here."

"Hold on, Isabella," Elsa said. She was creeping forward down the gloomy corridor, deciphering a panel across from the one that had Isabella engrossed. "I think we're about to encounter a puzzle path," she said.

"What's that?" David asked.

Isabella turned and stood next to Elsa, following the path of her light beam with her own. "It's what Elsa calls a booby-trapped path that requires knowing which stones to step on and which ones to avoid in order to stay alive, basically." She pointed to a set of hieroglyphics and murmuring something to Elsa, who shook her head and answered in an equally muted tone that Mukhtar was unable to distinguish.

A light shone behind them and he turned to see Moto, accompanied by another crewmember who was feeding an extension cord down the corridor behind them. Moto was carrying an air compressor with a hose and wand in his hand. He set it down on the dusty floor of the corridor.

Elsa and Isabella turned at their approach. "Oh, good," Isabella said.

"Yes, that's just what we need," Elsa agreed.

Mukhtar stepped forward and shone his light on the panel Elsa had discovered. He read it quickly and said, "It's astrological."

"It is!" Elsa said, obviously impressed with his skills.

"We need to blow the sand and dust off the floor so that we can see and decipher the symbols. Look." She shone her torch on the surface ahead. "Do you see the indented outlines in the dust? There's a network of stones that come together very much like a puzzle and certain stones are booby-trapped."

"With what?" David inquired.

"Never anything good," Elsa said.

"This group, the architects from this era, used anything from poison arrows shooting from a concealed panel in the walls, to giant boulders falling on your head and crushing you, entire walls coming down to block you inside until you starve or suffocate, or having the entire floor collapse with no way around it in order to access the rest of the tomb. That could cost us weeks as we built a platform across or around the collapsed flooring," Isabella explained.

"Buried alive? That doesn't sound very inviting. What about the pressurized air? Won't that trigger any traps?" David inquired.

"No, we don't hit the stones directly. We angle the wand and blow air across the surface of the stones, rather than focusing the pressure on any one stone."

"You haven't used one before?" Mukhtar questioned, watching him closely.

"No, we never ran across one of those on the few excavations I was lucky enough to attend. The whole puzzle floor aspect is fascinating!" David said, and Mukhtar believed him. His voice was animated, his body language tense and expectant. He shone the light across the walls, up and down, then back and forth between them, though he didn't seem able to understand them. Or was that an act? Could he in fact read them? Mukhtar wondered.

He stepped back to let Isabella access the equipment.

She turned on the machine and the dust on the floor vibrated and flew back. Pumping the trigger to test the amount of pressure the machine projected, she turned and began to expertly blow the sand and dust from the floor in front of them, jetting it to the edges and exposing individual stones wedged together in an intricate pattern, each stone bearing a unique symbol. Once she had cleared as many stones as the air pressure would reach, Isabella turned off the machine and stood back. Their ears continued to ring a few minutes after the loud motor stopped echoing off the stone walls.

"Those aren't astrological signs," Elsa said too loudly.

"No, but they're symbols for specific religious ceremonies or rituals, and those coincide with specific times of the year and thus specific astrological constellations would appear in the heavens at those times," Isabella said, her words growing softer as her ringing ears became accustomed to the now quiet cavern-like passage.

"Yes," Elsa said. Then, more softly, "Yes, you're right. Now all we have to do is decipher which ceremonies we need to use and which ones will kill us."

Mukhtar was impressed with Isabella's astute analysis, but decided to hurry things along as it was nearly nightfall. "Look at this section here," he said, studying the panel Elsa had been evaluating. "It's talking about putting away."

"Casting out, or, no, wait . . ." Isabella said, standing beside him and pointing to a particular hieroglyphic. "Casting in, hmm, containing, confining . . ."

"Gathering, or entrapment," Elsa said.

"That's it. It makes sense in the context. Here's Anubis, but he's not weighing a soul, he's not even taking the soul to the afterlife, he's entrapping it in a vessel."

"How does that make sense?" Elsa said. "Unless they're talking about the encasement of the organs in canopic jars."

"No, it definitely the soul. Look there," Isabella said, shining her light on another hieroglyph."

"A soul entrapped in a jar? They can't be talking about a Jinn, can they?"

"Why can't they?" David asked.

And something about the way he said it sent chills up Mukhtar's spine. But he couldn't see David's face because he had turned away from him and was flashing his light on the pathway.

"What would that have to do with Egyptian religious ceremonies? Except for King Solomon, centuries later, who performed ceremonies that involved Jinn?"

"Isis," Mukhtar said.

Isabella gasped. She waited for Prince Mukhtar to elaborate, but when he said nothing further, she turned to Elsa and said, "There is an ancient and little-known legend of Osiris and Isis condemning all unfit and unclean entities to the underworld, and that would certainly include Jinn."

David stepped forward and onto a stone.

"Wait," Elsa said.

"The puzzle is solved," he said, taking another step.

When nothing happened, Isabella said, "You've stepped on a harvest and a fertility ceremony symbol. How did you know they were relevant?"

"Growing, harvesting, breeding, all are related, like this one," he said, taking another step onto a pictograph of a phoenix that symbolized rebirth. "They all relate to controlling all life on earth."

Isabella saw no fault in his reasoning, and clearly he had deciphered the key since no traps were triggered, but she wondered at his tone and the almost defiant way he strode to the next stone. She stepped onto the first stone and then repeated his pattern, as he moved forward. When he turned to glance back at her, she caught his smile in her light beam and smiled back. She felt his protective warmth wash over her and the excitement of the hunt returned to surge her heartbeat and she stepped forward. Trusting in him completely, she hurried to catch up.

CHAPTER ELEVEN

sabella couldn't sleep.

She was too excited, and too frustrated. They'd made wonderful progress over the past week, and had finally reached the burial chamber only to discover another immoveable stone door they had not yet been able to open. She had internet access via satellite, and she'd been searching the online databases she had access to, seeking any other mention or record of the unfamiliar symbols she had found on the walls of the priest's tomb. Finding no such context, she sought whatever she could find on the Jinn. There was a great deal on that subject, since few Egyptians could be found who didn't believe in their existence, yet she was unable to find even a reference to the legend of Isis she knew to exist. She's read it, but now there was no trace of the document in which she'd first heard of it.

Elsa had given up and gone to bed an hour ago, so Isabella sat alone at the table. She stood up, stretched and tightened the belt on her robe before she took her coffee cup over to the microwave. She hit the 30 second reheat button and looked out the blind over the sink. A light coned along the ground just a few yards in front of her, moving toward the dig site. She rushed to the switch and turned off the overhead light, peeking out the blind over the side door. Whoever it was, they continued toward the tomb, striding with purpose but without hurry, as though they belonged and were unconcerned about detection or interference.

She reached to pull her handgun from the holster on the counter, grabbed a torch from the drawer next to the kitchen irons, quietly opened the door and slipped outside. A soft breeze ruffled the fronds in the palms that surrounded the oasis and muted the sounds coming from the furthest tent, open and stocked with coffee and a few of the prince's sentries. The moon was nearly full and combined with the closeness of the stars in such a remote area, she was able to see the way without her torch.

Running, her slippers silent on the sandy pathway, she chased after the light she's seen from her RV. It was probably another sentinel. Both David and Mukhtar had them, more alert than ever with the excavation open and well underway. But with their progress so close to her goal she had no intention of letting a stray thief come in and beat them to the treasure. What if those technology thieves had more friends and what if the technology equipment wasn't their only goal? How did David and the prince know all their own men were loyal? Isabella picked up her pace as disastrous possibilities continued to race through her mind.

The tarp set above the entrance came into view just as the light ahead of her disappeared and she realized that not only had whoever she was following entered the tomb, they had just turned the corner in the labyrinth of passageways that led to the burial chamber. Why would a sentinel enter except to steal whatever treasure they could find? But then, she reminded herself as she hurried down the first corridor, they still wouldn't know how to open the final door.

She came to the puzzle pathway and switched off her light. It was faster to be in the dark long enough to hop-scotch across the stones she had sprayed with promethium-chloride paint. Their luminous glow was more visible.

As she reached the end of the trap-laden stones, she switched her torch on and hurried around the corner, fuming that she had made it so easy for an intruder to find their way through the tomb's own theft deterrent system. The tunnel-like hallway was in darkness, which meant that whoever she was following had already reached the low passage that led downward to the burial chamber. Isabella switched her gun from safe to serious and rushed down the corridor and around the next turn. She thumbed her light off a moment and was immediately enveloped in complete darkness. It rushed at her on the damp, stale scent of lost eras. But even then the Egyptians had known what the smell of treasure could do to men, and had made appropriate precautions.

The thief, and she was now convinced that's who she chased, was already in the foyer outside the burial chamber, or she would have seen the glow of their lamp coming from the tunnel up ahead.

Switching her torch on, she moved warily, not wanting to betray her presence by even the faintest sound of pebble on stone beneath her soles. The path ahead, a rather uncertain and dubious one even when well lit, led downward quickly, requiring her to bend slightly at the knees and waist to safely work her way over the uneven rock. One slip, a trip, and she could easily have a dangerous, tumbling fall down the unforgiving rock slope.

The low tunnel was six foot in height so that both David and Mukhtar had been forced to duck while descending. It was no more than three feet wide, but seemed even more confined due to the steep incline. When she got about midway, Isabella began to watch for the gap in the wall. Elsa had rescued her from certain death earlier that day by grabbing her arm and pulling her back when she noted the indentation. Carefully stepping over the trigger stone that Elsa said would have sent arrows or darts or a spear, or some other form of poison-dipped weapon into her torso, she continued down the tunnel until she was a few feet from the bottom, then switched off her light. She paused for a moment, suddenly realizing the intruder hadn't triggered the device and wondering whether they had a lucky stride, detected the danger, or were a traitor within their own camp.

A faint glow summoned her attention. The intruder was only a few yards away, right around the corner. That put them in front of the burial chamber. Using her hand on the wall to steady herself, she crept downward until the tunnel broadened into a foyer, a much higher, squarish chamber with a twenty-foot radius.

Suddenly the ground beneath her feet trembled. She pressed against the wall and felt strong vibrations within the stone. They coincided with the grating sound of a weighty boulder sliding across a resistant surface littered with sand and dust. The noise echoed through the corridor with a deafening volume and gave her the opportunity she needed to lift her gun and launch herself around the corner to confront the intruder.

"Stop right there," she shouted breathlessly, sparking another surge of adrenaline as she realized she had just quoted every good-guy-maneuver-gone-bad movie she'd ever seen.

"Spoken like someone carrying a firearm," Prince Mukhtar said, raising his hands above his head and turning to face her. "Please don't shoot, Lady Isabella."

"Mukhtar? What are you doing here? How did you get the door open?"

"If you put away your no doubt loaded weapon, I'd be happy to explain."

"Very well, but stay where you are until I've heard what you have to say," she said, lowering her gun.

He nodded, and said, "Fair enough. It was bothering me, the fact that we couldn't get the door open despite the levers we found. So I continued to study the photos we took and search online databases trying to find some clue, something we had missed. And as you can see, I figured out the key and was too excited to wait until morning to test my theory."

"Obviously. So what was it? What were we doing wrong?" she asked, stepping forward in her own excitement, unable to squash her curiosity despite her mounting distrust of him.

"In a nutshell, we didn't realize there was a sequence to the symbols, and we weren't pressing the triggers in the correct order. There was probably a fail-safe, and it was only by luck that it didn't function properly, or one or all of us would be dead now."

"And you have obviously used the correct combination," she said softly. He nodded and smiled, lowering his arms. His eyes, and she suddenly realized it was her destiny to know them well, were large and expressive, set wide apart and sheltering under a still smooth brow, despite the desert sun, and arched over by thick, finely sculpted dark brows. The irises were of a baffling protean blue which was never twice the same. She had seen them run through many shades and colorings, like fine silk in sunshine--sometimes dark and brooding with the hopeless somberness of thunderclouds blocking the sun's light, and at other times grayish-blue, as chill as winter skies in England, and still other times, like now, they were a clear cerulean that reminded her of the Red Sea. They were eyes that masked his soul with a thousand guises, but she knew they sometimes opened at rare moments like this one and allowed it to rush up into the world for some wonderful adventure.

He moved closer and she felt winded as though she'd been running.

At first he said nothing, studying her face, gazing into her eyes with such intensity he might have been solving another riddle, but then he said, "Shall we take a look, as long as we're here?" Abruptly, startling her from her own fascination, he turned to swivel a halogen lantern he pulled from a hook on his belt around the cavernous chamber in which they were standing.

Isabella's breath caught and she sucked in a deeper one, shoving the gun in her pocket and lifting her torch to help illuminate the splendor. She felt like she was on an emotional coaster and each twist and turn brought heightened stimulation and awe.

"A favorite of Isis," Mukhtar said softly, as if to himself.

The walls and even the vaulted ceiling of the chamber were still resplendent with brightly colored murals, despite the centuries they had spent abandoned by time itself. The chalice, if it was present, was not the only treasure they were about to recover.

"It certainly looks that way," she said, turning slowly to take in the many sailing ships, bird hunting in the marshes, and domestic scenes, probably of the priest and his family. "He was certainly a high-ranking priest, so why do you think his tomb is located on what must surely have been his funerary lands meant to support his heirs and the upkeep of this very tomb, rather than nearer to the Valley of the Kings? This is an Old Kingdom tomb, I'm certain of it."

"It would have required special dispensation from Pharaoh himself," Mukhtar said.

There were numerous statues of richly-garbed Egyptians, their gods, and even a golden statue of a revered cat that resembled a modern Siamese. "Look there," he said, pointing to the far right. "Another chamber. Probably a ceremonial room. If the chalice is here, that would be its location."

"Why would the priest have stolen it? This is not the tomb of a thief."

"It seems more likely it was secreted here, and perhaps that is the reason his tomb is so far from the expected location, too. We may never know for sure," he said, walking to the door.

Isabella joined him. Noting a scarab carved into the wall to the left of the doorway, she reached out and pressed it. The door, rather than sliding to the side, rose into the ceiling of the threshold with very little sound save the soft whoosh of a vacuum exposed to air after millenniums of greeting only death as an occupant.

"I've never seen one of these in person. This tomb was designed by the same architects used to design the pharaoh's pyramids," Isabella said, feeling chills bump up her arms.

Mukhtar hurried forward and stopped in front of an ornate golden pedestal. Centered on the top was a golden chalice, intricately engraved with hieroglyphics and scenes they had already seen as petrography in the tomb's passageways. Reaching out to slowly turn the chalice without lifting it from the stand, Mukhtar revealed the scene on the back. It showed a wispy figure whose mist-like lower torso disappearing into an exaggerated, oversized gemstone ring on the finger of a figure seated on a throne-like chair and wearing a crown. It was not, however, King Solomon, but a shapely female figure wearing a crown upon which a coiled cobra rose up above her forehead. Another wrapped itself around her forearm.

"Isis," Isabella said softly. "So the legend is true. This chalice has something to do with the Jinn."

She glanced up at Mukhtar and when he looked down she could see her own joyous sense of accomplishment shining in his eyes. Despite her distrust and insecurity, it had begun to feel natural for her to bend her head together with his over a new discovery. Unlike David, who seemed almost manic in his sense of urgency to find the relic, Mukhtar enjoyed the hunt as much as she and Elsa.

His thrill over the find shifted. She sensed it, felt it herself, before she saw his eyes darken with raw desire. The attention he focused upon her was powerful and masculine, luring and compelling.

Mukhtar saw her, understood her, the young, lonely woman who was an independent individual, an archaeologist struggling to appear happy as a successful shop owner and failing miserably. She could feel suppressed desire ready to explode in him and her own rose up to meet it in synchronic celebration. They had both become so careful not to touch, not to let their hands reach for the same tool or brush away the same gathering of dust.

When he bent to kiss her, he paused, his lips hovering mere inches away, silently asking a question she was more than ready to answer.

She wouldn't, couldn't deny her feelings for him any longer and grasped the back of his neck, her fingers splaying through his hair as she drew his head down to savor their mutual passion. His mouth brushed over hers and then his lips parted and their breaths mingled, warm and expectant.

Had it only been a little over a week since he'd saved her from crocodiles and kiss-started this undeniable soul-tug she felt for him? His tongue slipped into her mouth and her eyes slid shut as he provoked more dangerous feelings. Heat pounded through her core with the fast-beat of her heart and she sucked air in through her nostrils, unwilling to break the joining of their lips and tongues and passion.

His hand traveled up from her waist and dipped through the gap of her terrycloth robe to caress her breast over the silk of her nightgown, his thumb teasing the nipple as he thrust his tongue deeper into her mouth. Her own met it eagerly and she leaned toward him. She felt a gentle tug and her robe parted.

The lamp now sat on the floor, freeing him to grasp her waist and draw her against himself. The slight chill of the tomb was quickly replaced by the scorching heat of Mukhtar's body. Lifting his head, he bent to kiss the sensitive flesh below her ear lobe. His lips pressed a moist trail along the curve of her neck, along her collarbone, and across the upper flesh of her left globe. His hand ran slowly down her back stroking her buttock before he smoothed her nightie down her upper thigh and darted his hand underneath the hemline only to caress its way back up her leg so it could linger on the firm rise above.

She sucked in air and breathed in rapid gulps from her mouth. His erection, assured and strong, pulsating with leadership abilities, throbbed against her abdomen and motivated her to embrace wanton thoughts and abandoned inhibitions. Her torch bounced on its rubber casing and rattled to a stop. Isabella unbuckled his belt and with a quick zip she reached into his pants to grasp his penis instead, stroking a groan from him as she demonstrated her own headstrong guidance.

He moved back and quickly stepped from his pants and boxers. Shrugging out of his outer robe, he turned to whip it out so that it bellowed briefly and then settled onto the ground like a blanket. When he turned back he stood immobile and naked before her, his attention traveling leisurely over the transparent film of her gown. Her own was just as captivated as she appreciated the most magnificent male specimen she had ever encountered. Apparently he too had begun preparing for bed and had left his shirt in his tent. Neither of them missed it or the robe that he helped her spread across his own after removing her weapon and placing it a safe distance away.

He ran his hands across her shoulders and snagged the thin straps with his thumbs, drawing them down her arms and watching the last of her nightwear skim down her curves and pool at her feet. She ran her hands up the shadowed hills and valleys of his abdomen, deliciously revealed by her abandoned light source.

His features appeared more chiseled and rugged in the diffused illumination, even more masculine if that were possible, which added a seductive element of mystery and anticipation to their encounter. He bent to recapture her mouth with this lips and tongue, and gently rubbed the fleshy part of his palm against her with ageless and expert rhythm.

She arched into his hand and moaned against his mouth, quivering, aching for release. Wet and ready for him, his finger moved inside her, coaxing her to completion, and when she pulled her mouth away, panting and murmuring mindless entreaties, he carried her down with him to their makeshift bed. Her second climax began slowly with mounting intensity and she sensed him reach away, then return to move above her. He parted her legs with the soft nudge of his knees, first one, and then the other.

A realization that he had sought and used protection made her smile softly as she reached out to pull him close, anxious for the earlier heft of his penis to fill her now.

Right now.

When he entered her, she wrapped her limbs around him and drew him deeper. He withdrew and she felt abandoned until his next trust filled her completely, over and over until it chased the spark of her previous orgasm and reignited her mindless pursuit of another.

He lifted his leg to straddle her and reached to grasp her leg. He shifted his weight and rolled to his back, bringing her with him again, this time astride his throbbing member. She leaned forward to adjust to the fit and rhythm and gazed down at him through the spill of her hair, still damp from her shower, but yet curling about her face with the proof of her current efforts.

He reached to tuck a strand behind her ear, as though he wished a better view of her face, and then squeezed her nipples and massaged them between his thumbs and forefingers until she threw her head back and cried out, "Oh, God, yes, again, please," and gyrated upon his shaft while flexing and releasing muscles she reserved for pumping hormones rather than iron.

She felt every titillated nerve ending and breathed in the fresh citrusy scent she now associated with him. Her lids fluttered shut as she felt him swell within her and he muttered, "May the gods protect me from you . . . and from myself," before he groaned long and deeply and buried himself in her hot juices. Isabella shuddered.

Then she collapsed, spent and content, upon this heaving chest and struggled to catch her breath, wondering at his words as well as his effect on her. It was too late to worry about the dangers she herself had undertaken by becoming the lover of a man she wasn't sure she could trust. The fact that she had such earth-shattering feelings for this man, and not just physical ones, made him even more dangerous.

His words only served to make her more fearful. Was he struggling against his feelings for her, too? And was it because he planned to betray her?

CHAPTER TWELVE

uhktar buried his nose in the intoxicating smell of her hair and hugged her against himself, savoring the afterglow of their union. He inhaled the faint fragrance of hyacinths and the sweeter, more enticing scent of Isabella's pheromones mixed with her sexual pleasure and felt an overwhelming desire to bond himself to this woman forever, to protect her from the hidden dangers she faced now or any future threat she may encounter. It was more than an impulse, like the one to kiss her that he'd had the first time he'd seen her. For the first time in his three decades he felt his soul drawn to a woman, and he'd been with more than his share. Too many, he suddenly realized. The idea of other women no longer had any appeal to him, and he admitted to himself that he'd thought of no one else since he'd first met Isabella.

A slight vibration pulled his attention away from the woman in his arms and he focused, trying to determine the source.

"The generator. Someone's coming," he said.

Isabella gasped and pushed against his chest as she hurried to disengage herself. They rushed to shake the dust from their clothing and get dressed. Glancing around the chamber and then at each other, they adopting a feigned sense of normalcy as the bare bulbs strung across the foyer coincided with the sound of their generator starting outside the burial chamber.

"You're right! The burial chamber's open," David said. "But she's not here, Elsa. Where could she have--"

Elsa gasped. "Am I dreaming?" she asked.

"I'm over here," Isabella called, walking into the outer chamber.

"Izzie! I was terrified. My knickers were in a dreadful bunch, but I just knew you had probably come down here, having deciphered the correct code. I just knew it! And there's another room? Is it filled with--" She stopped abruptly upon seeing Mukhtar follow Isabella into the room. "Prince Mukhtar . . . you helped too?"

"Yes," Isabella said quickly, before he could reply. "Another treasure hunter unable to sleep until he'd solved our riddle. It was Mukhtar who broke the code and managed to open the door. And yes, we found a ceremonial chamber over here and in it--"

"The chalice!" David exclaimed. His eyes sparkled in the light from the lanterns Mukhtar's men had gathered from the corner in the foyer and were now stringing on roped posts along the walls. "I'm so happy to see you here, safe and successful, Isabella." He placed his hand upon her shoulder, looked down at her and smiled in a way that was much more intimate than Mukhtar was comfortable seeing. "Elsa and I were both betting on you," he added with as much pride as a doting parent with a gifted child.

The soft glow in her cheeks told him that Isabella felt warmed by his rival's praise. David's trustworthiness was never in question for her, and his attentive support and protectiveness had given her confidence, a stronger set to her shoulders and a spring to her step. He'd become a true friend to both her and Elsa, and even to himself, Mukhtar admitted. It was easy to laugh and joke with the amicable man whose true preoccupation was obtaining the relic and an impressive reward.

Mukhtar knew the minute Isabella felt a surge of guilt at their shared lovemaking. She glanced away from David as if unable to meet his eyes which positively glowed with the man's affection and pride at her accomplishment. Whenever she was with David, she seemed to forget he existed. It was obvious that she felt a strong connection to her business partner that could easily go far beyond business. She craved David's attention and relished his approval. When he turned his kindness to someone else, she actually acted like a jealous school girl. It was like an obsession.

Mukhtar couldn't explain much less understand her feelings for David and how they affected the growing relationship she had with him. As far as he knew, and he'd made it his business to keep track, David had never even kissed her. So why was she acting like she'd cheated on him? Mukhtar had no doubt of her feelings for him, despite her reservations that they might prove ruinous to her. He knew she had heard about and disliked his reputation regarding women and openly voiced her fears that he may well intend to steal the relic or use the symbol on it to undercut her employer. She had voiced those fears to Elsa, but his men had overheard through the listening devices they'd planted in her RV and had informed him of her suspicions.

"Isabella? What's wrong?" David asked, obviously noting her distraction and discomfort at his scrutiny. "You did find the chalice, didn't you?"

"What? Yes, it's . . ."

She turned to point toward the room behind her and he didn't wait for her to finish, but dropped his hand from her shoulder and rushed past her to enter the ceremonial chamber.

"Ah, and here it is, just as you predicted, my dear Isabella."

He reached for the chalice and a trio of voices shouted, "No! Stop!"

"Don't remove it from the pedestal," Mukhtar warned.

His hands froze in midair. "A trap. Of course. I nearly forgot in my excitement." He turned to look at Isabella. "Have you found it?"

"We haven't had a chance."

He lowered his hands, took a deep breath, and glanced at the floor as if he'd known to look there. Mukhtar watched blood rush into Isabella's face as she saw David note the large, displaced dust pattern her and Mukhtar's robes had created as they made love. He glanced at Mukhtar. *A challenge?* And then looked back at Isabella, before saying with what Mukhtar sensed was forced pleasantness, "Yes, of course. You would not have had time. It's late. We can set guards within the tomb itself and begin fresh in the morning. What's one more evening? The important thing is that you found it."

"And also that you found all this!" Elsa said, indicating the treasures in the burial chamber.

"Yes, it's incredible that it's untouched, that no bandits ever managed to discover its whereabouts in all these centuries," Isabella agreed too quickly as if glad for the change of subject and the opportunity to think of something besides David and Mukhtar.

She walked to the corner and examined a mural image as Elsa began to flash photos with her cell phone. Mukhtar nodded and Moto stepped beside her and began to snap pictures from a more sophisticated digital camera.

"Thanks, Moto. Can you upload those to my cloud as you did the wall murals from the tunnels?"

"Of course, Lady Isabella. My pleasure," he said, "the prince has already instructed me to do so." He continued to make his way down the wall, his camera flashed photo after photo.

"If you see what I do, it would appear the chalice wasn't stolen after all," Mukhtar said over her shoulder.

She glanced back before returning her attention to the mural. "Then yes, I do see what you're seeing. Isis gave it to the priest, which also seems to prove your theory that this tomb was chosen as its resting place with the sole intention of keeping it hidden. But from who? What was its purpose?"

Turning, she looked up at him and said, "If you know, please tell me, now."

He wished for a moment that he could tell her everything, share with her joyfully the way they had joined together in their excitement over each new discovery and puzzle solved. But he had a duty and it was greater than any one man and his wants or needs. Giving her all he was honor-bound able to share, he said truthfully, "The engraving on the chalice itself holds the clue to solving that mystery, Isabella."

She looked toward the ceremonial chamber where David was still snapping his own photographs, of the chalice. He would probably send them to their employer as soon as he left the tomb and could get a satellite signal. Her bonus check was all but signed, which made Mukhtar feel guilty as hell.

He felt so confused and . . . worried? Premonition, of what he had no idea, was shooting tension up his spine and he felt cold of a sudden, like someone had walked across his own grave.

Pulling the collar of his robe up, he saw Isabella tug the edges of her own robe closer, and then she tightened the belt. Had the temperature dropped? No, not possible at this depth. Despite the added lights, the room seemed darker. The shadows cast by the assortment of statues fought against the light's intrusion until the bulbs flickered and dimmed, and once more they began to dominate the chamber. Popping sounds were followed by the distinct crackle of shattered glass as though an unseen hand was snuffing out what remained of the artificial illumination.

The sepulcher was filled with subtle movement as though the darkness had been awakened to their presence and resented it. He caught movement out of the corner of his eye, but when he spun to confront the attacker—and he now felt besieged by threat—no one and nothing was there. He sensed movement overhead, and looked up. Seeing nothing again, he fished his lantern from his belt and his gun from a cargo pocket on the side of his pant leg.

Stepping closer to Isabella, he looked over and noted that she too now held a gun. He was not imagining the threat, then, for she sensed it too. Another shadow, cat-like in appearance, darting along the far wall drew his attention. "Damn," he said softly.

"What's going on?" Isabella whispered, pressing up against his side.

He called out to his men in an ancient Bedouin language known only to them, unwilling to terrify the woman he loved. Pulling his necklace over his head, he held the talisman in the light of his lantern. The crystal prismed in the beam and reflected around the room as it spun on its gold chain.

Instantly a blur of shadows fled the chamber with a rush that sent his hair blowing, and then the bulbs revitalized. The entire energy of the crypt shifted and brightened. Isabella dashed forward. As he realized what she was doing, she rushed into the ceremonial chamber with him on her heels. The door swooshed shut between them. He reached out to jam his palm against the scarab, but nothing happened. He tried again. Again the lever sunk inward, but failed to activate the door's mechanism. "Isabella?!" he cried out, though he knew she would not be able to hear him through the eight inches of stone that separated them.

Moto appeared at his side, and he said, "Where's Elsa?" His lieutenant nodded toward the closed door. In there with David, Isabella, and the Chalice of Isis. "Let's hope they can find a fail-safe and activate it, or they might well suffocate."

"Emil and Rashad were in there too, so it looks like there's even less oxygen," another of his men said as he approached.

Mukhtar's hand clenched around the talisman that Prince Anubis had given him. He knew his men were right and that the group of people, though few, couldn't survive for long in the small chamber, but he couldn't bring himself to admit it.

CHAPTER THIRTEEN

What the bloody hell just happened?" Elsa cried in alarm.

That's when everyone's torch went out, leaving them in total blackness. Suddenly there was a grunt and the sound of flesh hitting flesh. Isabella backed against the closed door and froze, listening and shaking her torch, trying to get it to turn on.

"What are you doing? Stop! It's me, David. Ouch! Stop it!"

Scuffling feet and blows.

More fighting.

A gun went off, firing two rounds, and its flashes revealing Elsa crouched on the ground, her arms wrapped around her head, with David standing beside her, his arms raised to shield his face. The terrifying sound of ricochet reverberated around the room and then it stopped, suddenly, and she heard a gasp followed by a groan and then a thud as something, or rather someone, hit the floor.

"Elsa, are you okay? David?" she called, ducking down and making herself less of a target.

"It wasn't me," Elsa said.

"Or me, at least not yet," David added. "Stay down, Isabella!"

She thumbed the switch on her torch and gave it another shake and was shocked when it responded. Quickly pointing the beam toward Elsa and David, she breathed a sigh of relief to see them safe. Sweeping the room, she discovered two men, laying prone and still. She stood up and continued to illuminate the bloody sight before her.

Elsa stood up and grabbed David's arm. "You're bleeding. Your nose, David. Did someone hit you?" She glanced over at the scene in the cone of Isabella's light, froze, and started screaming.

Isabella took in a gulp of air, thankful that Elsa was vocalizing her own reaction, one that had stuck in her throat. It freed her immobile limbs and allowed her to run over to Elsa and hug her close. Relief flooded through her as David enfolded them both in his embrace.

"It's okay, Elsa. We're all safe. That's all that matters."

Her screams gave way to sobs and she grasped Isabella fiercely as though afraid to let go for fear something worse would occur.

As her sobs subsided, Isabella pulled away and turned toward David to ask, "What happened?"

He nodded toward the two men and said, "The prince's men. I'm afraid we turned against our boss's advice at our own peril. Your earlier doubts about Mukhtar were well founded. I'm sorry I urged you to trust him."

"What do you mean?" she asked, knowing her worst fears had been realized, but unwilling to admit it. Not now. Not after all he meant to her. But then, she wasn't the first woman to fall victim to a one-sided love affair, and she was sure this sharp ache in her chest would go away eventually, if she lived long enough.

"They were trying to kill me. Apparently the prince wants the artifact after all."

"Well at least you managed to stop them. Are they dead?" Elsa asked glancing toward the bodies and quickly looking away.

"They appear to be dead, yes. But it seems the prince is taking no chances. He has sealed the door behind you, Isabella, and unless we find another way out, we will shortly suffocate."

"You're right," Isabella said. Enraged to think she could have fallen for a man willing to kill her, she said, "Come on, Elsa, pull yourself together. Look there . . . your torch is working again. No idea what that's about, but the lights in the sepulcher were malfunctioning as well. Perhaps there's some sort of electrical field here. Now help me find another way out."

She moved to the wall behind David and began to carefully examine the mural from floor to ceiling, pressing her fingers against any area that seemed uneven, searching for a hidden lever or panel. David and Elsa began on two of the other three remaining walls, moving as quickly yet thoroughly as they were able.

Half an hour later, David called, "Here. I think this might be something, but one of you had better check in case there's a trap or the like."

The women hurried over to the wall behind the altar, examining the slight indentation David indicated. "Feel it," he said.

Isabella ran her finger along the seam until she couldn't reach any further. "The best revenge is success. I think you may have found a back door, David," she said, trying not to appear as excited as she felt. She ran her palm out horizontally, stopping when she found another seam. "Okay. Someone check over there."

"Got it," Elsa said, running both hands, palms down, to the right of the first seam while Isabella did the same to the left of the seam she'd just found. "I found it," Elsa exclaimed. "Ready?"

"More than."

Elsa pressed, and a round indentation appeared. She rotated her hand clockwise and the circle swiveled. The panel between them swung inward.

"A door," David said. "And air. Can you feel it?"

"Even better, we can breathe it," Elsa said, laughing.

"We need to get the chalice though."

"I've been thinking about that," Isabella said. "Step into the corridor. I have an idea. Oh, wait, can I borrow that," she said, reaching for the light in Elsa's hand. "And this," she said, pulling the scarf from her hair. She pushed them toward the corridor, ignoring the concerned look of confusion on their faces. Once they were out of the chamber, she pulled the door until it was only open a crack. "Now don't open the door until I tell you."

She shrugged off her robe and piled it carefully beside the pedestal. Flicking off Elsa's torch, she wrapped it securely in Elsa's scarf. Taking careful aim, she threw the cushioned torch at the chalice and ducked behind the altar. The light clanked against the metal, then a series of swooshes followed by the splinter of wood against stone sounded around the room. She waited a moment, then not hearing anything further she peeked cautiously over the top of the stone structure in front of her.

Seeing nothing more amiss, she glanced at the wall behind her, just above the surface of the altar. It was riddled with chipped paint and even a few splinters—what she suspected were poison darts-- that had managed to stick in the stone wall. They had projected from small holes around the perimeter of the pedestal beneath the chalice, triggered when it was removed. She shone her torch around the room and confirming that they had shot with force from every side of the pedestal. Reaching down, she picked the chalice up from where it had landed on her robe. A quick turn assured her that it was undamaged. Sitting it carefully upright on top of the altar, she slipped into her robe and grabbed the chalice and Elsa's scarf.

She swung open the door and held up the chalice. "I believe you were saying we needed this, David," she said, holding it out.

Rather than taking it, he clapped his hands together and said, "You are truly the queen of Egyptology!"

"What? Not the queen of Egypt?" she retorted, laughing.

"You're the queen of the world, right now," Elsa said, reaching to take the chalice and her scarf and rewrapping it.

"Here, I'll take that. You ladies lead the way. We've not escaped the tomb yet."

CHAPTER FOURTEEN

re all his men accounted for, Moto?"

"Yes, we found the other two sentries. They were down by the oasis drinking and playing dice rather than standing guard. They're all cuffed and under guard in the vans now."

"You explained it was for their own safety, until we sort out what's going on and who's to blame?" Moto nodded. "One less worry then. And at least Set hasn't gotten his hands on the chalice yet. Let's assume our team will find another way out."

"If not, they would have already run out of air," Rashid said.

"Thanks for pointing that out!" Mukhtar snapped. "Now go see that the men have staked out the entire perimeter. Who knows where they'll exit. We have to find them before Set can get his hands on them or the relic—which they will likely have brought with them."

"Yes, your highness. At once."

How could this have happened? Mukhtar fumed. But then he was certain it was Set and that he had used dark magic to keep them from getting to the chalice first. What he couldn't figure out was why Set hadn't waited until they had the relic and then tried to steal it. Why lock them in by sealing the room with the chalice? The answer seemed too obvious. He wanted to kill them, and he had probably intended to kill Mukhtar as well.

Having a sudden inspiration, he took the amulet from his neck and pressed it against the scarab. "Moto!" he called, as the door opened. Why hadn't he thought to try breaking the enchantment with the amulet earlier? He drew his gun and ran into the chamber, only to find it empty. No people and no relic. Relief that Isabella and the others were still alive rushed through him as he exhaled deeply. But then he flicked on his torch and noticed his fallen men.

Moto ran in and seeing the bloody bodies he said, "They killed our men? Do you suppose Set found another way in and ambushed them?"

"I--" In truth it hadn't even occurred to him, but it should have as it was a likely explanation. After all, what reason would David and the women have for killing his men?

He walked over and stooped down beside the crumpled body of Emil, a young cousin he had known since childhood. Reaching down to close his unseeing eyes, he took note of the bullet hole in the chest area of his shirt and the wide crimson stain that saturated the area around the wound and had soaked the sand beneath him. "Forgive me, Emil. I didn't know into what danger I was sending you."

Glancing over at his cousin's best friend, Rashad who had fallen beside him, he shook his head, feeling the full weight of their deaths. He felt Moto's hand on his shoulder, offering silent condolence for his grief. Taking a deep breath, he stood and said, "We need to get these men out of here. Have someone bring a couple of stretchers and enough men to take care of them. I'll call their families later myself, before their bodies arrive. Leave a crew in here to guard the rest of the relics. We need most of them with us, now. Set has somehow gotten past the sentries without being seen, probably with magic, and we need to make sure we find Isabella, David and Elsa before Set can get them off site."

"Yes," Moto said. If he manages to get them away from us, they probably won't survive."

It was his greatest fear.

*****

Mukhtar lay on his belly, night vision binoculars sweeping slowly from left to right, watching for any sign of movement. He had no way of knowing how long it had taken Set to find a way to kidnap David and the ladies, or how much time they had spent safely removing the chalice from the pedestal. They may not have been working their way through the tomb's inner tunnel system for long, but he couldn't take any chances. Why did he have his crew backhoe the sand from around the tomb? If not for that, Set wouldn't have been able to sneak past them to find a hidden passageway.

He battled his mounting anxiety, knowing that the longer it took them to emerge the less chance there was that they were unharmed. "Come on, Isabella," he said softly. "Where are you?"

His phone vibrated and he pulled it out and read the message. "Come on, Moto," he whispered. They saw something on the other side. "Let's go."

Slip-stepping down the sandy slope, Mukhtar ran to the wall and then along it until he reached her as she emerged from an open door about six feet from the ground. Her long hair had escaped its bands and reflected the moonlight like a beacon. His heart beat faster at the sight. "At last, Isabella! Are you safe? Turn and hang from the edge. I'll catch you when you let go," Mukhtar said, excited at the prospect of holding her safe in his arms again.

Isabella glanced down at him and disappeared within the open doorway. Confused, he waited for her to reappear. He saw movement, and focused his light. "David! Do you need help?"

"Move away, Mukhtar," he called. Then a shot sounded and the bullet kicked into the sand at his feet.

"Shit. What the hell, David?" He saw a man, and it wasn't possible to tell for sure in the darkness but he had at first thought it was David who leaned down and took aim, preparing to shoot again. So he ran, Moto at his heels, putting distance between them, sticking close to the wall to keep from providing a better target for whoever was shooting at them. Mukhtar could only imagine that Set or his minions were holding them hostage and warning him off.

Even if it meant failing at his mission he wasn't going to take a chance that anyone would hurt Isabella. She might have disappeared from view because someone pulled her away. Turning to look back once he determined they were out of direct range, he saw Isabella and Elsa running in the opposite direction.

Mukhtar stopped. David was behind them, glancing back over his shoulder to see if they were being pursued, but no one else was with them. There was no sign of Set or any of his minions, so no explanation for why the trio was fleeing.

Mukhtar grabbed his phone. Jamming his finger against a number he held it to his ear, not taking his eyes off the trio. "Stop them. No one is to get hurt, including you. They're armed and they're firing. Use the tranquilizers and stun them if you must. Just be sure you get the relic and no one gets hurt!"

"Let's go," he called to Moto and the half-dozen men who had run down the hill to meet them. Then he took off at a sprint, determined to get the relic as well as the woman he loved. He had no idea what was going on, but he fully intended to find out.

He reached the summit over which his targets had just climbed and looked around to get his bearing. The high beams of a Jeep ignited and revealed their former team members running toward David's Humvee. That vehicle's headlamps lit and a beep sounded as David pressed his key fob. They were still thirty yards away when a Land Rover cut them off, splaying sand as it spun to a stop between them and their goal. Two more vehicles slammed their brakes as they formed a semi-circle in front of them. The Jeep bumped past Mukhtar and rolled in behind them like a dog herding cattle. Another Jeep sped forward on the other side so that Mukhtar and his men on foot brought up the rear and closed the trap.

Isabella and Elsa stood back to back, turning in a circle in order to evaluate their situation. David spoke to them, and placed a hand on each woman's shoulder. When his men began spilling from the vehicles, guns drawn, the trio turned to confront Mukhtar. He shouted an order to his men and continued forward while his men held back.

"What is this?" Mukhtar asked. "We thought you'd been abducted. Clearly we were wrong, so why did you kill my men, and why are you running away with the chalice under cover of night? If you had changed your mind about our presence on your excavation, you had only to say so." He stopped when he was within three feet of them. His glance took in the women. Elsa looked frightened and conflicted, but Isabella was clearly angry and defiant, as though he had betrayed her, as though he were the one who had needlessly killed people she was close to, who she had known all her life.

The injustice of whatever misunderstanding had occurred reignited his own anger and he confronted David, who he now knew to be responsible and snapped, "Those men had families. They were a part of my family. It wasn't necessary to kill them in cold blood. They worked for me. They were here because of me. And it was I who had to call their families and try to explain. It was I who had to send home a body instead of a husband and father. Please explain these senseless murders, David. Explain why though I sent their brothers home with them to help comfort their grieving families, I should not exact their revenge myself. It is, as I am sure you realize, the way of the Bedouin, and of our clan in particular. I am honor bound to kill you."

"I'm well aware you wish to kill me, but you are mistaken, Prince Mukhtar," David said. "It wasn't murder. It was self-defense."

"What nonsense are you speaking? That's impossible. My men would never have harmed you. They were working with you as a part of your team and were under orders to follow your instructions, to help you in any way they could."

"I can't speak for their loyalty or intentions, only for their actions, and they did indeed attack us. I was defending these ladies as well as myself," he insisted.

Mukhtar looked at Isabella for confirmation and she said, "Stop the charade, Mukhtar. Just admit that you had every intention to steal the relic from the very beginning."

He swallowed. He couldn't bring himself to lie to her now, not now when he did indeed plan to do just that. "My men would never have attacked you. They have been instructed to protect you at all costs. Isabella, you know I would never let anyone hurt you. You can have all that is within the tomb, priceless antiquities, but the chalice, yes, that I must return to its rightful owner."

"It's rightful--" Isabella began.

"I knew you worked for that bitch. Another of her lapdogs. Illuminati, aren't you?" David spit, as though the very mention of the clandestine organization were distasteful, but his eyes in the glare of the headlamps looked wild, opened wide and darting about as though he saw danger all around him and was suddenly terrified and desperate. "Enough of this," he declared. Shoving Elsa so hard she cried out and fell to the ground, he grabbed Isabella and pulled her in front of himself like a shield, his arm around her throat. He pressed the business end of a Glock against her temple. "Since you have so kindly instructed your men not to harm her, order them to move."

He began to back away, dragging Isabella with him. Mukhtar raised his arms to wave off the men who had moved protectively closer at the sudden threat to her. His anger dissipated as he watched her expression shift from shock to fear before she began a quick back-step to keep up with her partner-turned-kidnapper and dug at his arm clamped against her windpipe in an attempt to ease her breathing.

Mukhtar kept pace, moving slowly and steadily forward, alert for any opportunity that didn't involve possible danger to Isabella. He prayed David was bluffing, but wasn't willing to risk Isabella's life weighed against the balance of the man's desperation. He had, after all, just revealed his allegiance with Set. How else would David know about Isis, or the fact that Mukhtar and his men were part of the Illuminati, a highly sophisticated, secret and impenetrable organization that fanned out from the immortals themselves through countless generations of devote followers who would lay down their very lives to protect and serve them, even from one of their own, the Usurper, Set.

When they reached his SUV, David backed past the front door and told Isabella to open it, and then half dragged and half carried her in with him. "You drive," Mukhtar heard him say before the door slammed shut behind him.

He ran forward, but seeing David's gun still pressed snuggly against the fair hair at Isabella's temple, he watched helplessly as the vehicle started up and began to pull away.

"What is your will, my prince? My men can take out the tires. It would slow them down, even if he continued to drive the rims across the sands."

"Contact the men doing surveillance on Set and his minions. Take them out. All of them." He clamped his teeth together, took a deep breath, and said, "Now! They can't orchestrate an exchange if their contacts are dead." He opened his mouth to say more and froze. A thought not his own nudged his consciousness and he felt an immediate sense of relief to know the cavalry was truly on its way and that it was Horus and not Horus's mother, Queen Isis, who was about to communicate with him telepathically.

***

"Come now, Elsa, just tell us what David said to you and Isabella just before we caught up to you. I saw him. He had his hand on your shoulder and he leaned down to speak to you. What did he say?"

"I don't remember," she said again.

"It might save Isabella's life, Elsa!"

"Her life's in no danger. He-he--" Suddenly, she burst into tears, crying uncontrollably.

"I'm sure she's fine, Elsa. Truly. We are doing all we can to get her back safely."

He handed her a tissue and pushed his hand through his hair. They were getting nowhere with her. She just wouldn't cooperate and seemed to genuinely believe she was helping protect Isabella with her silence. What could have gone so terribly wrong that they felt he would harm them? What had David said to convince them he was a threat? Surely after what they'd been to each other, after . . . maybe she had been using him.

"I-I can't believe he just left me behind like that, pushed aside like so much garbage," Elsa sputtered, blowing her nose for emphasis. "I thought he loved me, but he was just playing me all along. He really wanted Izzie!" she wailed, off on another crying jag.

Mukhtar just stared at her, dumb founded. Elsa and David? Why hadn't he known about that? His men should have seen something. But Isabella and David? Then why would she . . . Elsa wasn't the only one who had been played.

"Do you mean to tell me that Isabella went with him willingly? It was all a ruse?"

She nodded affirmatively, causing a vice to tighten around his heart before she took another tissue from the box he held out and loudly blew her nose. "He told us to play along, to just follow his lead." Sniffles. More blowing. "And then he just pushed me away!" Hysterical tears.

He sighed, handed the box of tissue to one of his men and exited the RV. A helicopter sounded overhead, and he jogged toward the area past camp, holding the edge of his robe up to shield his eyes from the displaced sand flapping around the aircraft in stinging sheets as it hovered over the desert floor before landing. Moto ran up beside him and handed him a pair of night goggles, which he accepted thankfully.

"It's Prince Horus," Moto said, though he knew the aeronautic company logo on the helicopter would have made it obvious.

"Yes, come on, we're going with him," Mukhtar said, ducking and running with his personal guard beneath the slow-whirring blades toward the door opening at the rear of the large craft.

He climbed aboard and took the empty seat next to the prince while his men clambered around filling whatever other seats were available as quickly as possible because the craft was airborne again before they had even fastened their seatbelts.

"Good to see you, Prince Mukhtar. I hadn't thought to see you again until the next scheduled training camp. My men get lazy until shortly before they know you will be bringing your men to kick their asses," Prince Horus shouted over the sound of the engine and the whirling blades. He chuckled amicably.

Mukhtar nodded, fisted his hand over his heart and bowed his head politely. "I wish it were better circumstances, your highness. I owe you my humble apologies for having failed in my mission. It was a honor to have the queen entrust me with this assignment, and I--"

"Nonsense, my friend. You have no need. I of all people know what a badass you are, but none of us expect you to go against the evil forces of the Jinn unassisted. This was actually my father's doing. Nothing happens in Egypt without him hearing of it, but he should have realized the evil bastard would seek whatever could send him back to the underworld for good."

"Ornias is here?"

Horus nodded.

Of course, it made perfect sense, Mukhtar thought. The shadows in the sepulcher, not dark magic, at least not the form he had thought. Jinn. Moving so quickly he was unable to distinguish them. Locking the chamber, breaking the lights so they were unable to be seen. And unable to maintain their mist-like form in the presence of the amulet. Why hadn't he realized it? Of course Ornias would send his own army against them. So where was he now?

"Where's Isabella?"

"Down there," Horus said, pointing out the window as the helicopter descended.

CHAPTER FIFTEEN

Isabella blinked. Her head was tilted at an odd angle, leaning between the window and the headrest. She sat up and tried to twist the kink out, turning her head from side to side. What happened? Had they been in an accident? She gasped and looked over at David. He was slumped over, his bangs hanging down so that she wasn't able to see his face.

"David? David!" Her words seemed to come from far away, they were so faint. She leaned toward him and was jerked back by the seatbelt. "Dammit," she said, reaching to snap the release button. This time she was able to nudge his arm, and gave it a gentle tug. "David, wake up."

He groaned. Alive then, she thought, and sighed with relief. She didn't recall an accident, but of course there must have been one. Her neck was still tight and her left shoulder where it had been pressed against the door felt sore, but other than that she wasn't injured.

Suddenly, as she became fully conscious, she was aware of the reason her voice seemed so faint. It was overwhelmed by the storm surrounding them. The Humvee was besieged with gusts of wind until it felt as though it might turn upon its side. Sand blasted against the sides, obscuring any view the headlights would have provided through the windows. A sandstorm then, but why had they lost consciousness? They must have turned over.

"What's happening? Where are we?"

"Thank goodness. Are you hurt?"

"I-I don't think so. I feel hung over, sluggish. I can't seem to remember anything."

"I think we had an accident."

The wind died down and the sand still swirled but stopped its perpetual blasting. It was then they both heard the ch-up, ch-up, ch-up, ch-up of a helicopter overhead.

"What the hell's going on?" Isabella reached to open the door. When the handle wouldn't budge, she pulled up on the lock and yanked the handle again. It still wouldn't lift. "Try your door," she shouted at David. "They're going to kill us!"

"Who's going to kill us?" He tugged on the handle and shoved his shoulder against the door. Then he pressed the window lever, but it just hummed away without lowering the glass.

"The prince and his men. Surely you remember that they're trying to get the relic from us?" She looked at the floor by his feet, turned to switch on the dome light and pointed. "Elsa's scarf. Quick, check to make sure the artifact is still inside."

"We have the chalice?"

"You've forgotten that too?"

He bent down and picked up the object wrapped in soft pink cashmere. Unwinding the scarf, he revealed the engraved, golden vessel. "Beautiful," he said, slowly turning it in his hands. "Interesting scene on the back. Isn't that what the prince--"

His door flew open, they were both blinded by a powerful halogen beam shining in their faces, and a hand reached in to snatch the chalice before either of them could react. "Hey! Give that back!"

David yelled. He leapt from the vehicle in pursuit, but was grabbed by two Bedouins and held struggling between them.

Isabella's door sprang outward and Mukhtar appeared beside her. "Come with me," he shouted above the racket caused by the helicopter. His hand around her arm assured her it was not a request. She swung her legs out and jumped down. Before she was fully erect she felt her gun being pulled from the pocket of her robe. Jerking her arm out of his hand, she snapped, "I suppose you'll use it to shoot me now."

He didn't respond, but she could see his anger in the stiffness of his posture. His face was covered by the end of his kuffiyah which he had tucked into his golden agal. Even his eyes were veiled by the night goggles he wore, while she squinted against the sting of the swirling sand.

"Here," he said, handing her a kuffiyah. She hooded it over her head to help protect her eyes, wrapping the corners around her neck to secure it. The Humvee's headlamps were on, and combined with the assortment of torches and the aircraft's slow-rotating blades the light and shadow played across the sand in a kaleidoscope pattern that made her feel dizzy and disoriented.

When Mukhtar grasped her arm she didn't fight him, but let him lead her to the helicopter. She had little choice but to climb in and settle into a seat beside David, who was already inside. He reached over to squeeze her hand reassuringly.

It didn't work.

She took in her surroundings, the double row of highly-armed soldier types, including Mukhtar's Bedouins, weren't smiling, and all seemed overly alert to her and David's presence. She looked across the aisle. One of the tallest men she had ever seen sat next to Mukhtar. Even seated she could tell that the man had to be nearly seven foot. His impressive breadth of shoulder fit his height and he exuded strength, in as excellent physical condition as Mukhtar. She didn't see how she could have forgotten had she ever met him, but he seemed vaguely familiar. His military-like khakis bore some sort of emblem on the pocket, but she was unable to make it out in the dim interior of the craft--other than to note that several of the other men on board were dressed in similar fashion. He wore his hair short, which rather than making him look stern made him look rakishly handsome, the sort of wild-fun bad boy everyone's mother warned them about and every father forbid them to date. She quickly looked away when he caught her staring and smiled at her.

The huge helicopter lifted and then took off, the sound deafening. She placed her hands over her ears and then accepted the earphones the Bedouin on her right held out toward her. Until he handed her a bottle of water, she hadn't realized how thirsty she was. She drained half before lowering the bottle to draw air.

She looked at Mukhtar, who was still wearing goggles. She couldn't tell if he was looking back, but his head was turned in her direction and it certainly felt as though he was boring a hole through her. She was much less concerned about staring at him. He had made a fool out of her for the relic and she had no intention of acting as if she were the one in the wrong. The relic. She glanced around at the other men, looking for the pink scarf. It was in the firm grip of a man two seats from the good-looking tall man who was now talking into a headset and had that relaxed yet confident bearing of someone used to being in charge.

The man with the relic was dressed differently from the others. If she didn't know better, she would think he was a priest. A Catholic priest. But what would a priest be doing with men involved in stealing a relic? Mukhtar's earlier claim that he had to return the chalice to its rightful owner nagged at her, but she dismissed it as an empty excuse by a deceitful man. She let her anger return to keep the fear of what they intended to do with her at bay. She would have demanded that the Italian-looking man stop masquerading as a man of the cloth, but it was too loud and clearly stupid for her to demand they return the relic at this point.

Surprised, she glanced toward the window though it was still too dark for her to have seen anything, even if she were close enough. It didn't require vision, however, to tell that the helicopter was already landing.

Were they returning to the dig? Why? Were they planning to steal the rest of the artifacts as long as they were at it? And what were they going to do with her? For that matter, what had they done with Elsa? She felt a rush of shame that she was only now thinking of her best friend's welfare. Why had David left her behind? The event came back to her in a flash and she realized the last thing she remembered was slamming her foot against the gas pedal to put as much distance as possible between them.

***

"David! At last! They've been questioning you for over two hours--" Isabella began.

"Why did you do it, David? Why did you leave me behind?" Elsa cried.

"I didn't. What I mean is, I don't remember doing it," David said. He moved to put his hands on her shoulders and looked down at her. "I never would have done something like what Mukhtar said I did to you, or," he glanced at Isabella, "to Isabella. I'm so sorry, for whatever I may have done."

"What are you saying? When you said you didn't remember getting the relic . . . what all *do* you remember, David?" Isabella asked.

"I'll try to explain, but do you think I could have a cup of espresso first? My head is splitting and I've been over all of this for the past two hours with Mukhtar and Prince Horus."

"I'll get it," Elsa volunteered.

"That's who that is!" Isabella said. "I knew I recognized that man. He owns that aeronautics company, Solaris, among other things. He's a multi-millionaire. What would he be doing here?"

"I believe he's actually a billionaire, and apparently this artifact belongs to his mother. I overheard Mukhtar talking to him when Moto was questioning me."

"His mother? I don't recall ever hearing anything at all about him having any family outside his wife and children. Who is she?"

"And how could she own an artifact that's been buried in this tomb for thousands of years?" Elsa added, handing David the coffee she had just pulled from the pod machine.

David smiled his thanks at Elsa, who beamed back at him, having apparently already accepted his apology without need of explanation.

"Would you like another cup, Izzie?" she asked.

"No thanks."

"Come, then, let's all sit down. David looks about to collapse."

Elsa was right. The bulb lamp over the table might not have been flattering, and none of them had been to bed yet and it was now dawn, but David looked as though he's just awoken from a six month coma. Isabella slid into the bench seat across from him and Elsa, feeling even more worried.

"What's the last thing you remember, David?" she asked.

"Hearing a commotion and discovering those men fleeing with our equipment."

Elsa sucked in her breath and placed a hand on David's arm. "You don't remember anything about the dig?"

"Not even discovering that Mukhtar and I had entered the sepulcher without you? You seemed pretty animated when you thought we had found the chalice," Isabella pointed out.

"I don't even remember discovering the tomb itself," David said. He rubbed his eyes and took a hard swallow of his coffee. "The harder I try to recall the more my head aches, but I still don't remember a thing. It's like I was asleep for the past ten, or was it eleven days?"

"My God, David. We need to get you to a doctor. Did you hit your head or maybe one of those thieves knocked you out." Elsa suggested.

"Elsa's right--"

A rap on the door. Moto stepped inside. "Lady Isabella, would you please come with me."

Knowing it wasn't a request, however politely presented, she stood up without speaking. David got up to join her and Moto said, "Just Lady Isabella, for now. You should try to get some sleep, David. You're exhausted."

"Yes, do, David," she said, placing her hand on his arm. "Elsa, make sure he does. He can use my bed."

"No, I--"

"What use will you be to us if you collapse? You can barely stand. I'm sure I'll be fine and back soon enough to get some rest myself."

"Yes, since you put it that way. I do feel exhausted, and can't think straight any more. Just a nap, perhaps."

Isabella nodded and smiled. "I'll be back soon," she said to Elsa, who still looked worried. "Just tend to David."

As she preceded Moto from the RV, she felt a tightening in her stomach and wished she felt half as self-assured as she had just pretended.

Moto pointed to the left and she walked silently alongside as he led her to a vehicle she didn't recognize but assumed belonged to Prince Horus since it bore the Solaris symbol on its side. It was one of the largest RV's she had ever seen. It was at least the size of an eighteen-wheel truck. The door opened at her approach and when she stepped inside, she was awestruck by the technological command center that confronted her.

Everywhere there appeared blinking lights and recessed screens with radar and satellite feeds, some of them appearing world-wide, and numerous video feeds. She even saw their camp, the crypt, the ceremonial room, and the oasis revealed on various screens. To her left she saw at least a dozen uniformed Solaris employees seated at acrylic tables, working on laptops, speaking to persons apparently off site on headsets, or monitoring the wall of data coming in from all over the globe. At the rear she noticed a door and assumed it led to the living quarters. So this is how one runs an empire from wherever one happens to be, she thought, looking to her right. Mukhtar was seated on a plush leather couch across from Prince Horus, who was on a cell phone. He stood and gazed at her with a look she didn't recognize on his face.

Moto held his hand out, indicating that she should join them.

As she approached, she heard Prince Horus say, "Later this evening then. Yes. I love you too," before he pressed his cell off and stood to greet her. Mukhtar made the introductions, they exchanged courtesies and then she sat on the curve of the enormous sofa, between the two royals who seemed as at ease with one another as brothers. Clearly they had known each other for some time.

"We spoke to your partner, David, at length, as I'm sure you know. His memory lapse was obviously not feigned, so naturally we were concerned."

"As are we. You should let us take him to a doctor immediately!"

"With rest he will be fine, and there is nothing any doctor can do for him, I'm afraid."

"How would you know? Are you a doctor?"

"No," Prince Horus said, his deep, pleasant tone unchanged, despite her harsh words. "But one of our doctors has already examined him, just to be sure my diagnosis was correct and that nothing else was physically wrong with him."

"Your diagnosis?" she asked, with more sarcasm than inquiry in her tone. She was powerless and a prisoner on her own dig site, and it made her angrier than she'd been when her father was killed because he was so excited to acquire a famous artifact he ignored the tell-tale signs of a tomb's theft deterrent system. He was crushed by falling rocks. His casket was closed and she hadn't even been able to tell him goodbye properly. She felt the same frustrated rage now, the same sense of betrayal and abandonment—though she probably didn't have the right to feel Mukhtar owned her anything at all. They had only known each other a couple weeks. It wasn't possible to fall in love with someone that soon.

So why did it hurt so much?

She looked toward Mukhtar, who was looking at Horus. Neither of them had answered her question and they seemed to be communicating to one another right now, though neither of them was speaking. Looking back and forth between them, Isabella's impatience grew until they seemed to sense her mounting anger and both turned to look at her.

Mukhtar stood and said quickly, "I would like to speak with you in private, Isabella. There is much I must explain."

Standing to face him, she snapped, "The understatement of all time. By all means, I'd love to hear you try to talk your way out of this bloody mess."

He sighed as though bracing himself against her harsh words or those yet to come, and said softly, "This way, please." Walking around the U-shaped couch to a door she hadn't noticed, built into the wall as it was, he pushed it open and stepped aside to let her precede him.

Lights ignited down the sides of the aisle, ropes of it along the carpeting of the walkway and recessed bulbs overhead, above each of three rows of captain's chairs, complete with arm rests and seatbelts, behind the driver and copilot seats of the vehicle. He sat in the end seat of the first row and swiveled the chair toward the aisle. She did the same opposite him, suddenly nervous to be alone with him though she had been dying for the opportunity to vent her anger and give him the set down he deserved.

Now, face to face with him, she swallowed her heart back down into her chest, digging her nails into the padded arm rests in an attempt to steel herself against her emotions and his. Tears welled, unwelcome, in her eyes and she still couldn't blind herself to how handsome he was, his shoulder-length hair curling behind his ears where she knew he'd shoved it with a careless gesture she'd once found so sexy, and his squarish jaw set in a firm line she already knew reflected his unwavering sense of determination and responsibility, but her downfall was the intensity of his gaze and those beautiful blue eyes, dark and brooding at the moment, with an inner turmoil that both confused and disarmed her. Why didn't he just say something?

"Isabella. I hardly know where to begin."

Dammit, why did the sound of her name on his lips still make her heart skip a beat? She should hate him. She did hate him.

She wanted to hate him.

CHAPTER SIXTEEN

How could he ever make her understand? She was so angry tears glistened in her eyes. He didn't blame her. Hadn't he purposely ingratiated himself into her expedition with the sole purpose of stealing her treasure? And hadn't he seduced her, to help secure her cooperation? At least that's how it started. In the end, he had lost himself in the warmth of her smile, the sparkle of excitement in her eyes, the scent of her hair and the taste of her lips. He closed his eyes, took a deep breath and opened his eyes to study her expression, hoping for even a small hint that she might ever forgive him. The drawn brow, fierce glare and the way her teeth kept chewing her bottom lip, probably to keep from telling him how much she despised him, made his heart sink into dejected disappointment.

"Perhaps if you asked me whatever questions you must surely have. I will answer them as honestly as I can."

"Honesty isn't something I have come to associate with what you have to say."

"I'm sorry, Isabella. I know I wasn't honest with you. It wasn't something I took lightly, especially after--"

"Don't dare speak to me of what happened between us." She glanced away, then back, looking him in the eye, her stare steely with tempered rage.

"Perhaps you would like me to explain about David?"

Her expression softened and he could see her sudden concern for a man he once considered a rival in the way her breathing slowed and how she moved forward in her chair, awaiting his next words attentively. "What about David?" she asked softly.

"The reason he doesn't remember anything from the night the men fled from your caravan is that--"

"Do you mean the thieves, the men David hired in Cairo who were trying to steal our equipment?"

"That's the thing, they weren't thieves and they weren't trying to steal your equipment. They were fleeing, but they were running for their lives. We've found four bodies, buried in the sand within the campsite."

"What the hell are you talking about? Who killed them?"

"David."

Isabella jumped to her feet. "More lies!" she cried her hands clenched into fists. "David would never do that. Did you tell him he had killed these men? That must have been a nice surprise!"

Mukhtar stood and raised his hands, palms up. "Please. I understand how hard this will be to believe, but let me finish explaining first."

She chewed at her lip, then plopped down in the chair and crossed her legs, her foot tapping her impatience against the carpet.

Mukhtar settled across from her. He knew it was going to be difficult, but she was too angry to listen. If only he had more time. But he didn't. If he wanted a chance, however slight, to convince her to believe the truth, to accept it, to accept and forgive him, he must do it now. He pushed his hair back and shoved it behind his ears.

"Isabella, please listen to all I have to say. Then I will answer any remaining questions as best as I can, and offer proof if I must."

She remained silent, her foot still rising and falling, but in a slower, less agitated rhythm. Feeling slightly encouraged, he plunged forward. "David wasn't conscious of that he was doing. It was his body, yes, but he can't be held responsible for his actions during those events or much of the time since then, I'm afraid. He was possessed." When Isabella clicked her tongue against the top of her palette, he raised his hand and said, "Please, just let me finish." She shrugged as though indifferent, and he said, "Let me backtrack a little. The chalice, you need to know what it's for."

"So you did know. Well, at least I knew that was a lie when you said it."

He looked down and then nodded slowly. "It wasn't my secret to tell."

"And now it is?"

"Yes," he said, looking her straight in the eye. "The prince has given me permission to tell you. To tell you everything."

"Why?"

"Because I love you."

"Stop it. Just stop it!" This time she jumped to her feet and when he stood, she shoved him so hard he nearly fell back into his seat. He caught her hands and pulled them into his chest to keep her from pummeling him. She tugged away until finally realizing he could hold her imprisoned against himself indefinitely, at which point she burst into tears.

It was his undoing. He couldn't bear to see her so unhappy, knowing it was entirely his fault. His guilt at thinking she had used him, played him while involved with David weighed heavily on him.

Horus had explained to him that she had been mesmerized by Ornias, who had taken over David's body, which is probably why he liked David so much, too. He felt ashamed to have been fooled by the very Jinn they were trying to capture with the chalice.

He wrapped his arms around Isabella and drew her close, smoothing his hand down her silky hair. "I'm so sorry, Isabella. So very, very sorry. Please forgive me."

She continued to sob, and when she pushed against his chest again, he let her go. He turned to pull a box of tissue from the console and handed it to her. It seemed he was forever helping females blow their noses. She took one and blew, and then took another and wiped at her eyes. Getting herself under control, she said softly, "How can you pretend to love me when you set me up for failure, with every intention of leaving my business and my reputation in ruins?"

"Oh, no, my dear, that is the one thing I would never have done, no matter what. Your employer, the anonymous phone contact, is incognito for a reason. He's a power-hungry monster, our most diabolical enemy, and he wants the chalice because it can be used to trap and control Ornias, an evil Jinn who tricks desperate victims into becoming his slaves."

"I-I have heard about the Jinn and even did a bit of research on them. Nearly everyone in Cairo, as you know, believes in them. But I never believed the stories I heard about human possession. So . . . so they're true?"

She was listening and asking questions. Mukhtar tried not to get too hopeful. "Yes, quite true."

"David, when he was not truly David, just before he pretended to kidnap me . . ." She paused and thought a moment. "I guess he actually was using me to get away. Did he, is it possible he thought you wouldn't harm me, even to get the artifact? You really do care about me, don't you? I-I thought you were going to leave me, that you were only using me."

The hopeful look in her eyes mirrored his heart. He bent to capture her lips and drank long and deeply of her willing forgiveness.

Raising his head, he took a deep breath and smiled at her. "Is it possible that you have feelings for me, too?"

"Would I have forgiven you for all I've been through if I didn't? I thought you only pretended to care about me so you could get the artifact. I couldn't bear the thought of someone else leaving me. I-I felt so betrayed."

"There's much I need to explain, and it will be hard for you to believe."

"Wait. David said you were part of the Illuminati, and that you worked for . . . the Chalice of Isis . . . no, there's no way that's possible."

"Much you think is impossible is not only possible but true. I need you to not only believe what I am going to tell you, but to trust me and be willing to keep my secrets as your own."

"I-I need to learn to trust again, but it's not going to be easy for me. What if I can't?"

"I'll help you," he said, pulling her back into his arms. "And I will spend my life proving that you made the right decision." He pressed kisses against her neck until she moaned, and then working his way back to her lips.

"Trusting you feels good, Mukhtar," she breathed against his lips.

CHAPTER SEVENTEEN

sabella pulled the hood of her jacket up and pressed closer to Mukhtar's side. He wrapped his arm around her. It was chilly in the ceremonial chamber. The flickering candlelight from what looked like a hundred flames were scattered around the room on candelabra, pedestals and even clustered on the floor. They rippled the shadows but failed to displace them. Most were focused around the area surrounding the altar upon which the chalice now rested.

The man she had mistaken for a Jesuit was chanting in a language much older and longer dead than Latin, head bent, palms pressed together as though in prayer, with a talisman rather than a crucifix wrapped around his wrist and dangling before him. A young man beside him used a taper with which he lit whatever elements had been added to the chalice.

A spell, Isabella thought. The man was not a priest, he was a wizard of some kind. But then she recalled that the rituals from today's religions originated from what some considered more primitive traditions. Magic and alchemy were among them. She watched with fascination as flames shot out of the chalice and then receded. Fragrant smoke that reminded her of frankincense ignited with dragon's blood billowed toward the high ceilings.

Isabella felt excited, and frightened. The ritual might even predate the tomb. She'd never seen an ancient Egyptian ceremony, but she'd read enough about them to realize that's what this was. Mukhtar told her she was about to witness the truth. It's what the chalice was intended for. He did indeed belong to the Illuminati. The rumors only hinted at reality. Ancient immortals the Egyptians thought of as long-forgotten gods founded the Illuminati as a secret society to help hide their continued existence. How was that possible?

Suddenly a disturbance caught her attention. A swirling shadow, wispy and ethereal circled the altar. It billowed like a snapped sheet and then the wizard-priest increased his chanting. The specter materialized slowly, solidifying from shadowy mist to a gigantic man with ebony skin, wings and horns, and fiery red eyes-fierce and angry. He bellowed with rage, cursing in multiple languages, all of them ancient, though Isabella understood them well enough to know he was not happy to have been summoned. She didn't need an introduction to realize she was looking at the Jinn, Ornias, the most evil and deadly of all the Jinn. He was called the soul-eater because the vampire-like fangs he revealed as he snarled his rage were used to suck the soul from the darkest, most wicked dregs of humanity upon which he feasted.

"Long past time for you to go home, Ornias," Prince Horus said from the far side of the altar. He held out his hand upon which a large golden ring with a large stone that sparkled in the candlelight gleamed.

"Noooo!" cried Ornias. "You stole that from Jasmine!"

The sound echoed around the chamber, seeming to grow in volume. Isabella gasped and covered her ears.

Prince Horus shouted, "She was happy to part with it, but you stole it from King Solomon's treasure chest." Then he issued a command and Ornias began to dematerialize. Soon he was once again a swirling mist. The vapor coned like a tornado and appeared to be sucked into the gemstone on the ring where it disappeared as though it had never existed.

Isabella blinked and inhaled deeply, realizing she had been holding her breath. Mukhtar turned toward her and reached under her chin to turn her face upward.

"Any remaining doubts?" he asked quietly.

She shook her head, unable to find words while she continued to process what she had seen.

"You must give me your final answer soon," he said.

***

"Our feline-focused boss is so happy with the pictures I sent him of the cat statue he told me he is doubling our bonus. And between Elsa's contacts through the museum and mine in New York we will have the rest of the relics sold before we even get back to Cairo," David said, giving Elsa a quick hug in his excitement.

"This is the shortest excavation we've ever been on together, Isabella," Elsa said.

"And one I bet you wish had lasted longer," she teased, nodding toward David.

David laughed and said, "I had my doubts about your prince, but he has proved invaluable. With the help of his men and equipment, the relics are almost all packed and loaded onto the trucks. I need to get back down there. I just came up to answer some phone calls since there's no reception down there."

"I'll be down shortly. I need to finalize a few things with Mukhtar first," Isabella said.

"Take your time. I'll drag Elsa back down with me to help supervise the last of the packing. At the rate we're moving, we'll be ready to leave by noon."

Isabella nodded and followed them toward the door, but Mukhtar was waiting and she stepped back to let him enter after David and Elsa left.

He pulled the door closed behind him and grasped her hand, moving toward the table. She slid into the seat across from him, smiling.

"You know why I've come."

"Yes, I know," she said before switching subjects. "I can't believe how completely Elsa and David have forgotten everything, including the existence of the chalice, or that they believe we came here for that golden cat statue. It's amazing really. I was worried about playing dumb and not saying anything with all the questions I imagined they would have. But they have none. Tell me something, if I hadn't agreed to keep your secrets would you have let Prince Horus wipe my memory as well?"

"No, of course not."

"And if I don't agree to marry you, will you be forced to let him do so?"

He stood up and moved to her side of the table, sliding in beside her as she scooted to make room. Taking her hand and raising it to his lips, he kissed it and then looked deeply into her eyes and said, "If you don't agree to marry me, I will die from a broken heart."

"You didn't answer my question, Mukhtar."

"What good would the knowing do you if you never wanted to see me again?"

"I take that as a yes."

"You surely understand the need for secrecy and even with all the precautions in place, even you have heard the rumors, though in fact many of those are purposely started by the Illuminati and their operatives to keep suspicion and speculation rife so that no one ever actually knows what to believe."

"Yes, I suppose the mystery and urban legend, the conspiracy theories all work to make people skeptical. Even knowing I have a difficult time believing it, and I have a strong suspicion that there's a great deal more I don't yet know."

"No one ever accused you of being stupid," he said, chuckling.

"Not even when I thought you were the bad guy?"

"Not even then. So are you going to answer me?" He moved from the table to bend down upon one knee and said, "I believe this is the custom in your country." Reaching into his pocket, he pulled out a large, oval emerald ring and reached for her hand. "Once again, with a sincere and loving heart, I most humbly beg you to become my wife, Lady Isabella Valentine."

Isabella stared at the largest emerald she had ever seen, shocked to suddenly realize that she had no idea what it would be like to be married to someone so incredibly wealthy, let alone a royal. Her father had only been a Lord and even then was forced to attend to certain family duties in England on occasion. Besides his duties with the Illuminati, what other duties must Mukhtar surely have? Rather than thrilling her woman's loving heart, the incredibly valuable ring made her nervous, scared even.

"Am I so undesirable then?" he asked.

She nearly laughed at the look of dejection on his handsome face. Surely he knew how many women would give anything to be in her shoes right now. "I have one last question first, and it's a serious one."

"Anything."

"If I were to say yes and become the first wife that you have, would you expect to follow one of your country's customs and have other wives, too?"

"I would have neither time nor desire to have any other wife but you, Isabella. All my time would be devoted to making love with you and keeping you safe from rampant Jinn."

"Promise?"

"For all eternity," he said, pulling her hand to his chest.

"In that case, I accept," she said.

He slid the ring on her finger and said, "You have made me the happiest of men, and if this ring had even a tiny influence on your decision, it was worth having one of my men fly home to seek it from my father who had given it to my mother. After she passed away, it was meant for me to give it to my bride one day, but it pales in comparison to your emerald eyes.

Isabella looked down at the ring, flashing green fire in the sunlight coming in through the open blinds. She slid from the booth and onto his knee, sealing their engagement with a kiss. It began slowly, her lips moving gently over his, light and teasing, but he wrapped his arms around her and deepened the kiss until she was breathless and wanting more. Much more.

Raising her head to take a breath she said, "Lock the door. Let's get started on our next adventure."

"Your wish is my command, fair princess," he said, and hurried to comply.

ABOUT THE AUTHOR

Her grown children have decided to remain in the frozen north of Michigan, so Elizabeth has flown from the nest and retired from her "normal" day jobs to live with her personal editor and Social Media VP, Hudson (AKA Maltese), and her husband, Kenton (AKA Irish-Scotsman), in the foothills of the beautiful Santa Catalina Mountain Range in Oro Valley, AZ, a decision she has never regretted.

She loves to entertain friends and family from colder climates, or hike the mountain trails, ride her bike or jog on the endless miles of bike/jog/walk trails, sit on her patio watching the local wildlife visit her private Sonoran Desert oasis, sipping coffee or wine and reading, writing, editing, or brainstorming plots, and enjoying the grandeur of her breathtaking mountain views. She can't imagine living anywhere else, because as she often tells her friends from far away, why not live in a postcard every day?

Keep up with Elizabeth and Hudson at: www.elizabethalsobrooks.com

Free Excerpt Enclosed

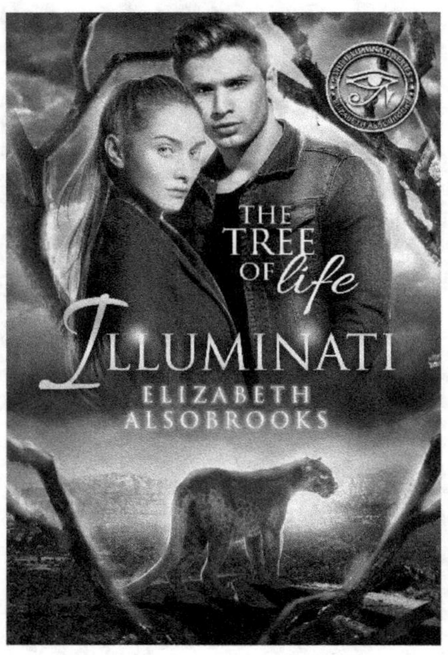

Kirin, daughter of Isis and Osiris, is an immortal. The only daughter of Isis in a family of older, brawny, warrior brothers, she has been taught to protect herself, but has also been fiercely protected and cherished. As a brilliant geneticist who has spent hundreds of years trying to unravel the secrets lost by their ancient ancestors, Kirin searches for the source of their immortality so they can reverse the genetic disorders their ancestors' experiments introduced to the human race. She hopes to wipe out disease and retard aging, but also realizes that unless she can find a cure, any of the mutants who have escaped the underworld must be captured and imprisoned to protect the rest of humanity.

Rio (Rodrigo) is a descendent of one such experiment gone awry. A black jaguar shapeshifter, he is able to read minds and beguile the will of others with this thoughts. He is not immortal, but his line lives centuries rather than decades. They have come a long way since their curse was first forced upon their family. Once they were not able to control their shifting and spent each night as a creature. Slowly over the years, their human nature dominated their animal side. Then, with the help of science, their family began to experiment with genetics. Now Rio has taken up the research and though he has nearly tamed the beast within him, using it for his own purposes, he has not yet found a way to cure the genetic mutation that afflicts his family tree—or exacted revenge on the immortals who cursed them.

PROLOGUE

The night air undulated, drunken, soggy with tumbling vapors. Fog surged upward and then interspersed with heavier moisture it swirled around the base of crypts and crumbling statuary. Precipitation was slow but steady, forming rivulets on the bows of umbrellas held above stooped heads. It snaked down massive tree limbs, fed moss-covered stones and coaxed tears from guardian angels carved into marble walls that flanked the ancient family mausoleum.

Mourners disappeared into the dark interior, and two silhouettes separated themselves from the deeper shadows of an adjacent oak. Refusing to be comforted, the small one pulled away from her brother's comforting arm and took a step toward the gravely pathway between the crowded sepulchers. Damp moss blocked her progress. Moved by increasing winds, tendrils swept the ground of the graveyard like a ghost trailing ragged skirts.

"Luc, how will I ever face him? I might have prevented this. She's the last of his line."

"It's not your fault, Kirin. You have done all you could," he assured her, reaching out to draw her back against his side.

"I'm so close now. If only…I have to save Sabina, before it's too late."

...and on either side of the river, was there the tree of life, which bare twelve manner of fruits, and yielded her fruit every month: and the leaves of the tree were for the healing of the nations.

--Revelations 22: 2

CHAPTER ONE

"Stop pushing me behind you," Kirin whispered, crowding against Luc's side in an attempt to see past him.

Brothers! They *allowed* her to accompany them. And even then it was only because she was the only one who could identify the specimen stolen right out of her own laboratory. She actually had every right to be involved. How dare those bastards steal it right from under her nose!

As if sensing her agitation, Andrew reached for her. Too late. A quick slip past Andrew's grasping hand. A fast dart under Luc's arm, and Kirin ran around the corner, elbowed the guard in the throat, and snatched the pass card clipped to his pocket before he landed face-down on the floor at her feet. She slid it through the reader, reached for the door handle and gasped.

Dangling a full foot above the granite-tiled hallway, she grit her teeth and kicked backward. She connected with her brother's shin. A grunt sounded. She grinned.

Carried over the threshold, she was unceremoniously dropped. Landing with the dexterity of a cat, crouched and on her feet, she curled a strand of red hair behind her ear. *Okay, I might have deserved that,* she admitted to herself.

Kirin ignored her brother's soft sound of irritation, and rose slowly and with quiet dignity beside Andrew's frowning attempt at towering intimidation and glanced around the lab.

Only half the overhead fluorescents were lit, but there was plenty of recessed lighting around the outer walls. Row upon row of fire-proof tile counters were inlaid with the occasional sink, protected by overhead fume-vented hoods and equipped with random Bunsen pilot burners, and under-counter stools. Colorful chemicals, solutions and solvents in beakers, crucibles, and vials bubbled, flowed, and dripped amidst scales, microscopes, hot plates, and auxiliary lighting. Here and there small work stations housed comfortable swivel chairs and evidence of more permanent, personal supplies, including networked computer access and electrical outlets. It was obviously a well-staffed and highly functioning lab during normal working hours.

Seeing an environmentally controlled storage room, Kirin pointed a gold-lacquered nail toward two doors at the far side of the chemical lab and signaled for her brothers to check there while she hurried in the opposite direction.

That's when she heard it. Wheels spun, a chair whirled into the aisle in her path and a startled white-lab-coated man half-rose to his feet. Kirin promptly tripped over his size twelves, toppled into his lap, and their momentum carried them both down the last three feet of corridor where the swirling chair toppled, casters still spinning, and deposited them both onto the sterile, polished floor.

Kirin, shocked, frustrated, planted her forearms into his chest and rising up glared into orbs as golden as a jungle cat's.

She opened her mouth to demand that he…what? That thought was lost to pure sensory reaction. Unusual in color and intensity, intelligent and curious eyes stared straight back into hers. And his scent. He smelled clean and fresh, like a warm summer's day. Her scientist's nose immediately dissected the aroma of spices, ancient, some sacred in their origins, with underpinnings of frankincense, labdanum and myrrh. She knew he was mortal, but somehow the fragrance suited him. *Why am I so drawn to this human?* Kirin wondered. His chest was wide and well-muscled beneath her hands. He didn't spend all his time in the lab. When the air whooshed from his lungs, she knew it wasn't entirely due to her elbows against his diaphragm. He felt something for her as well.

He licked his lips. They were full, sensual for a man. Perfect for giving kisses. When they curved into dimples, her gaze flew upward. One dark eyebrow lifted knowingly. Warmth flooded her cheeks even as she reminded herself this was the scientist whose work she had admired for years. Kirin planted her feet firmly on the floor, wishing she had reacted more quickly.

Instead, she was once again lifted off the floor by one of her brothers, but this time it was Luc and he was helping her up rather than trying to keep her from interfering.

"Hey! Who are you--" began Dr. Rodrigo Silva, as he scrambled to his knees. Unfortunately that's as far as he got before her famous right hook clipped him on the chin and landed him flat on his back, unconscious.

"Luc! No! What did you do that for?"

Luc shrugged off the obvious, righted the chair the scientist had conveniently vacated and pushed it back to the computer the young Brazilian had been working on. It lit up and Luc shoved a thumb drive into an open slot so he could bypass security codes and upload a virus.

"Fine. Don't answer me. Clocking the poor guy is easier than explaining that we're actually trying to save him from himself and just trying to retrieve stolen property."

When he continued with his task, she spun on her heels and headed back to the sample lab, adding, "He has to know what that sample is for. Why else would they have stolen it? That means we're going to have to take him with us so we can find out what he knows. So now someone will have to carry him."

"Fine," Luc said softly, but she heard him anyway.

Glancing back, she took in his expression and decided against further conversation. The slight rise of Luc's eyebrow sent a much different message than Rodrigo's. Kirin hurried to the storage room. She pulled open the door. Past numerous sample drawers, she headed straight for the key pad at the rear of the small, refrigerated room. A punch of the security code and she stepped back and waited as the depressurized vacuum seal released vapor and frigid air into the already chill room. A tug of the handle and she freed the pharmaceutical vault casing. Seeing what she sought almost at once, she grabbed the vial, shoved the lid closed and turned to find Luc standing in the doorway watching her.

"Got it," she told him, noting that he had a portable transportation case open and waiting to accept the vial. He nodded, deposited the sample in the transport and shoved it into an inside pocket and stepped aside to let her pass.

The handsome young scientist with the strong, sturdy chin, despite Luc's abuse and a two-day growth of beard, was introduced to her brother Andrew. Tossing the limp scientist over his shoulder, Andrew motioned for Luc to lead the way and followed them into the hall.

Once they reached the entrance, Andrew jogged through the door held open by their head of security, Roscoe, who along with several other men stood watch over the bound and duct-taped security guards in the lobby. "You've only got two minutes until the surveillance cameras come back online," Roscoe warned. Without wasting time to respond the entire team ran to the street and piled into a small RV with tinted windows waiting at the curb.

The siblings quickly shed their coats, revealing sophisticated if elaborately embellished evening attire, and donned artisan-created masks. Kirin fastened the second dangle diamond-and-emerald earring and then pulled on gem-stone-and-sequin-beaded gloves and watched as two of their men switched the scientist's white lab coat for a tuxedo jacket, slapped a bowtie around his neck and a mask over his face, covering the bruise swell on his chin.

Just then the man began to push against the mask and muttered, "Wha-what's going on? Whe-where am I?"

Roscoe lifted the mask, reached forward and held a cloth against the now struggling man's mouth. "Easy, Cinderella, you're about to go to The Magic Ball."

The van pulled around the corner and stopped near an emergency vehicle only zone, beside a long, dark limo with smoky windows and diplomatic flags on the hood that allowed it to park anywhere, even in Rio. The party-goers, along with their once-more-docile guest, quickly transferred vehicles.

Ten minutes later, as they pulled to a stop in front of the Copacabana Palace Hotel, Kirin chuckled. "Well, this should be interesting--us, him, and fifteen-thousand of our closest friends."

"Let's hope it's less an adventure than you predict, Kirin," Andrew said. The door swung open and he pressed the mask more securely against his face. He stepped out, and turned his head to look around. On the opposite side of the vehicle, Luc exited, nodding at him. Andrew reached down to offer his hand to Kirin. "Come, little sister, time to attend your favorite party. This better work. It's our only chance to get him out of here without getting caught."

Her ruby-glossed lips turned upward beneath her half-mask, and she teased, "Always the pessimist, Andrew. You used to be so much more fun when we were kids." Taking his hand, she swung her legs from the car. Once her glitter-gold stilettos clicked to the pavement Kirin rose to stand aside so he could haul her *date* to his feet.

To his credit, the man managed to stand with little assistance from Andrew, who threw an arm across his shoulder companionably. He swayed slightly and Kirin moved against his other side, wrapping her arm around his waist intimately, giggled and said loud enough for the attentive doormen to hear, "I knew you shouldn't have had that last martini, darling, the night's still young."

They were soon flanked by Luc and his men. The group entered the over-crowded hotel lobby, and surged up the carpeted marble steps, clearing a way toward the elevator.

"What's going on?"

Oh, you're back once again. You look great in a tuxedo, by the way," said Kirin. "I didn't realize you were so tall."

"First time you've seen him upright," Roscoe offered, helpfully.

Molten gold signaled his anger from behind the oval eye-slits of the full face mask Roscoe secured to the scientist with knotted ribbons, letting them know that if nothing else the man recalled the security chief's remark and harsh treatment from earlier, and that the effects of the drug-soaked cloth were beginning to wear off.

"Move," Andrew urged in a harsh whisper, shouldering the tightly grasped man in the opposite direction. Kirin looked up and noted that their security team averted them from the elevators and the assumed safety of their penthouse suites, instead directing them further up the massive marble staircase toward the ballroom, unmindful of the rumpled flounces and disgruntled minglers they jostled in their haste to make way through the crush of excited party guests.

She instantly sobered and followed her brother's lead, knowing their route must surely be blocked, probably by some previously off-duty revelers who just happened to be on site. But for their enemy to have discovered their whereabouts so quickly could mean only one thing--her blind date was more valuable to their enemy than they realized and was carrying a tracking device. He would need to be searched, and soon.

"It's him. It's got to be him," Andrew growled, shoving the man forward hard enough to carry Kirin along for the ride, her stilettos tapping a fast-step as she caught herself on the polished, art deco landing.

She apologized in Portuguese to the man whose drink she sloshed with her ungraceful arrival. Then, grasping the scientist's hand, she shouted through the increasing blare of the music, voices and clapping, "Come, dear. We must not keep the Samba King waiting," and began weaving her way through the throng of exotically costumed and plumaged A-listers. If she knew anything it was how to hide among garish delight.

The tall stranger was still off-center enough from the hallucinogenic afterglow that he held tight to her hand. It was the only clear direction in the midst of an undulating sea of primary-colored chaos. He stayed close behind as she wove her way through the throng of bystanders and then darted straight onto the dance floor, swinging around to clasp him against herself, and then spin away to the flash-paced rhythm of a Brazilian Samba.

"I'll explain later. I'm sorry, but if you want to get out of here alive, follow my lead," she shouted into Rodrigo's ear as she gyrated in front of him.

"Shouldn't I be leading?" he quipped, surprising Kirin by raising her hand above her head and spinning her away, then quickly pulling her back against him and showing off some amazingly sensual moves for a man who spent much of his life in front of a microscope.

He's awake! She searched the crowd for her brothers, who at 6' 4" and 6' 6" were usually easy to track. Luc was on the far side of the room with Roscoe, a stranger between them who they appeared to be escorting toward an exit. The scientist pulled her up against his chest, nearly knocking her breath away, and not just because she was surprised by his sudden movement. The gleaming challenge in his eyes bore into hers as he looked down at her. *If only he really were my date*, she thought for a fleeting moment of self-indulgence.

She imagined the mocking smile behind his mask, and she met his swiveling pelvis with her own sashaying hips, daring him to continue the knee-pumping, core-flexing duel. Encouraged, he stalked her movements like a predator, the fluidity of his tilt-and-pivot hip-swings measured and seductive. Kirin, breathless and impressed, laughed up at her handsome captive.

But then, a spin and a room scan revealed Andrew, headed straight for her. Just a few push and shoves behind him came several men she was sure hadn't received invitations.

"They've found us. We've got to get out of here," she shouted into his ear, then grabbed his hand and dashed through the gyrating dancers, dodging far-flung arms, kicking feet, and spinning bodies. Spotting an exit sign, she raced to the stairwell and fled behind the metal door, her bewildered date in tow.

"Who's found us?" he demanded, though he continued to race up the stairs behind her. "Wait! They're probably trying to rescue me!" he reasoned.

"I'm afraid not, Dr. Silva. They won't take the chance that you may tell us what you know."

"What the hell are you talking about? Wait, you know who I am?"

She spun at the corner and started up another flight of stairs. "Come on, Rodrigo, don't you think we know about the human trials you've been running?"

"Human trials?" he cried, angry, out of breath, still running at her heels.

"Yes, and just because you're hiding your poor victims away in the middle of the jungle doesn't mean no one knows what catastrophic mistakes you've made in your quest to obtain immortality."

"Immortality?" He stopped then, his incredulous disbelief hanging between them like a first-date pregnancy revelation. Hands on hips, he declared, "That's not even possible. Who's researching immortality?"

With little choice, despite their critical circumstances, Kirin turned to face him. "We may not have handled this well. I didn't even know you were working tonight, but we planned to warn you about--"

Ping! The metal handrail beside him sparked. He jerked his hand back. The bullet ricocheted, hit the cement block behind him, and caused them both to flinch. It sprayed glass as it buried itself just past his right shoulder in an emergency fire hose box.

"Shit! Keep going," he said, and this time he was the one urging her up the stairs.

Kirin grabbed the door at the top of the landing, jerked it open and breathed a sigh of relief. The guards were still in the penthouse lobby. Still secure. "Come on, this way!" she directed, then raced across the foyer to the door opened for her by one of their men. "Inside. Now!" Toward one of the guards, she called out, "They're on our heels," before they raced inside.

She hurried down the short flight of steps and then turned right toward the hallway. "Down here," she said, running into the bedroom at the end of the hall. Opening the top drawer of an antique English dresser, she pulled out a .45 and released the safety.

"What are you going to do?" he asked, taking a step back.

"Try to keep us alive," she said. Turning, she sat on the edge of the bed, put the gun down beside her and toe-to-heeled off her stilettos while she pulled off her gloves and mask.

"I've already seen your face, so you're either already planning to kill me or you don't care if I know who you are. Which is it?"

"Oh, I was never going to kill you, doctor. I've been admiring your work for years. That is until you decided to begin testing your formula on human subjects before it was ready. Now you have become a bigger threat to humanity than the ancients. I'm both surprised and more than a little disappointed in you."

"The ancients?"

"Never mind. We don't have time for that now. I'll explain later. Here, hold this," she said, thrusting the gun into his hand. "I have to change my clothes."

"What?"

She ignored his look of confusion, rummaged through the drawers and grabbed out what she needed. Arms full, she turned her back to him and said, "Would you mind?" Once he had unzipped her dress with what she noticed was rather nimble ease, she rushed into the bathroom. She let the dress, heavy with thousands of sparkling sequins and beads spill to the marble tiled floor around her feet, stepped out of the gleaming seafoam puddle, picked it up and tucked it over a towel rack. Then, stockings and garters removed, she replaced them with a much more comfortable pair of faded and well-loved jeans, and topped them off with a wine-colored hi-tech-fabric button shirt with short sleeves. A few quick brush strokes and she secured her thick, wavy red tresses with a pink elastic-scrunched ribbon.

Back in the bedroom, she sat on the bed once again and asked, "No unusual noises or intruders?"

"How would I know friend from foe? As far as I'm concerned you're not to be trusted. You kidnapped me."

"That's fair. I can see where that would seem to make me the villain, but I assure you that isn't true," she said, shrugging. "We're actually saving you." Reaching down, she picked up a high-top hiking boot, pushed her foot into it, jeans tucked inside, and repeated the process with the other foot, before crisscrossing the laces through the lancelets and tying them snug.

Sudden commotion in the foyer dissolved her casual attitude. She quickly reclaimed her weapon, having noted that given the chance Rodrigo hadn't turned the weapon on her, so on some level he trusted that she wasn't his enemy. With a hand signal, she motioned Rodrigo away from the door.

"Kirin? Kirin? Where are you?"

"I'm here," she said, opening the door and walking out into the hallway.

Andrew hurried toward her and glanced down at her change of clothing. "Good idea," he said, before shifting his attention to the man behind her. "Did you get the tracer off him yet?"

Tell-Tale Publishing would like to thank you for your purchase. If you would like to read more from this or other of our fine authors, please visit our website at:

www.tell-talepublishing.com